PAGES OF YOUR LIFE

THE SECRET LIFE OF SHIRLEY RUMMING

SECRETS: BOOK ONE

LEANNE WOOD

PAGES OF YOUR LIFE —

THE SECRET LIFE OF SHIRLEY RUMMING

ISBN eBook: 978-0-9953804-0-0

ISBN Print: 978-0-9953804-1-7

Book 1: Secrets Trilogy

Secrets

1. Pages Of Your Life - The Secret Life of Shirley
Rumming
2. Travels Through My Mind
3. Where Secrets Lie

For those I love and those who have experienced depression.

Never underestimate your acts of kindness and how much you are appreciated and loved.

PREFACE

Shirley Rumming was born in Sydney, Australia on 15th September 1924. She was an only child and throughout her life, she experienced the effects of both war and depression. Her world is turned upside down at a young age and she feels lost by all the atrocities around her, by all the hatred, the anger and all the despair. What will become of her, what will the future hold?

This is Shirley's story, a story that was not uncovered until after her death. As you read the pages before you, you will enter Shirley's world. You will share her experiences, her joy and happiness, her loneliness and sadness and she will reveal more than you could ever imagine.

CHAPTER ONE

Dear Claire,

The reading of this letter symbolises my passing; I want you to know that as your mother, everything I did or did not do, said or did not say, was in your best interests.

Throughout your life you looked to me for love, guidance and assistance and as your mother I believe I succeeded and that played an important factor in the closeness of our relationship.

After reading my book I hope you do not feel betrayed by my silence and I pray that you can find it in your heart to forgive me. The only way I felt I was able to protect you was to keep silent, I know this is no time for evasions, denials or excuses, and I fully accept responsibility.

I am truly sorry for my actions. Without either the strength or the guts to admit to my wrongdoing my past actions have taunted me constantly. I do not like what I have done but now as I stand in the truth of who I am I find peace in this truth and finally I am able to love myself.

It was very hard for me to write this book, as I had never mentioned much of its revealing content previously, to you or anyone else. I do not expect you to understand what I have done in my life and I know you may find some details almost impossible to believe.

LEANNE WOOD

Please forgive me, I never wanted to hurt you, for you are the one person who I truly loved, you will always be my "sunshine."

> *You are the light from the moon,*
> *The sparkle from the stars,*
> *The warmth from the sun,*
> *And the colours in the flowers,*

> *I thank you for being a loving daughter.*

> *With all my love*
> *MumX X X*

CHAPTER TWO

Many people say we are born into this world with nothing and our future is what we make of it, determined by the actions we choose and the paths we take. Others say, our future is destined by fate, already mapped out for us, planned by a higher being, a God if you like. I am not sure if either one of these theories could be discounted. My feeling is there are many paths set before us, like lines on a road map, all leading to one final destination, but how we get there, well - that all depends.

Take William Smith. Nicknamed Bugsy, after the large set of choppers, which could not fully be contained within his mouth. He was born in 1921, in a small town called Dunberry, which at that time travelling by car was five hours North West of Sydney and had a population of not more than six hundred. The first born son to a local farmer whose family had been working the land for generations. It was expected fate would see Bugsy working the land just as his father did and his fore fathers before had done so. On the day he was born his parents, Jack and wife Beatrice had been over the moon, of course a baby girl would have also made them as happy as punch. But a boy! What they saw before them was a baby boy who would in time make a fine young man to carry on the family farming way.

Within minutes of the first feeding time at the hospital they had discussed and mapped out what they saw as their son's life - his fate.He would go to the local school, which at that time educated fewer than twenty students of mixed ages and abilities, all within the same classroom. At the age of sixteen, he would travel to Sunnyside Boarding College. Where he would learn all theories relating to the latest farming technology. Once these studies were completed, two years later he would return to take over his father's role, with all the wisdom the world could offer.

To his parents, William Smith would have a long and happy life, once returning from College he would work side by side with his father. Learning all the family farming secrets and practicalities, they fail to teach at College. After a few years, he would not only be wise enough but strong enough to handle whatever nature dealt him.

He would meet a nice local girl. They would date for a period until he declared his undying love for her; they would marry, he would continue to work the farm. She would cook, clean and take care of the house. Later she would fall pregnant and bear him a child, William junior, who would in turn carry on the family farming tradition.

My family did not hold a background in farming; instead we had always been referred to as city folk and had first arrived to Australia in the 1800's as free settlers. The decision to move to Australia was both daunting and frightening, a decision which could not be taken lightly.

* * *

My great grandfather, on my father's side was a skilled carpenter, at the age of twenty-five he had a wife and two young children, a son Frederick and a daughter, Edna. Although, he held what was considered a safe job that paid well as the economic depression swept Europe the ground below everyone's feet was becoming unstable. He had to be realistic, should he stay within the safety of his own comfort zone where his future was not guaranteed or should he take his life with both hands and thrust him and his family into the great unknown.

For years, my great grandfather had secretly desired more for his family, what he wanted to gain from life was a higher fulfilment, a balance of life with his family. Australia offered what he believed was an authentic life.

Stories of wealth, cheap land and work opportunities were like dangling a carrot in front of a horse. Australia was looking for good British workers to fill vacant land; the preference included married couples with children, my great grandfather fit all the criteria, but would he take such a daring step.

Starting from scratch would require a new challenge in confidence; he had to question if the decision to move would be viewed as selfish. Not wanting to make the decision alone he discussed all options with his wife. Sometimes, in life you can not plan and control everything, England was changing, as the depression grew deeper, more and more found themselves out of work and plummeting into famine.

The voyage, they acknowledged, would mean they would have to endure months at sea. However, they would be leaving a very gloomy and uncertain England for the promise of a better and more prosperous life, one with the possibility of endless work and cheap land on which they could build a bright future. On the other hand Australia was also considered a strange and hostile land, plagued by torrid heat, by droughts, bushfires, torrential rain, floods and fierce Aboriginals.

Life was a gamble, full of so many uncertainties, both agreed if the move wasn't to be taken for their own sake then they had to muster the courage for the future of their young children, Fred and Edna. With the consensus and support of my great grandmother my great grandfather took the plunge and attended the Government Inspectors Office to obtain the required medical clearance. And that is how my family hit a crisis in confidence, stood by their decision and first came to Australia as free settlers in 1874.

These great grandparents were dead long ago. So from a young age I knew the oldest living member in our family was their daughter Edna, my father's mother, the old battleaxe, who lived alone in the Blue Mountains at Faulconbridge. She was somewhat a recluse; a grumpy old snapping bitch, who rarely had a kind word about anyone. Her only friend, an old grey longhaired tabby cat with one eye called Fummy. I hated it when we visited her and I don't believe she enjoyed it either. Rarely were our visits welcomed by an endearing smile and there was never any "Lovely to see you," greeting. More so, we would be subject to verbal abuse even prior to her opening the front door.

"Get off my porch or I will kick your nose through your arse," she would bellow.

My father responding, "It's just us mum we have come for a visit."

Her house was always so dark, closed up and musty smelling. The carpet sticky beneath your feet from God knows what. There she would sit in her lounge chair, like the bloody Queen on her throne barking out orders and slanging off about whoever and whatever subject arose. Continually stroking Fummy, cat fur whisking up into the air, covering her clothes, and giving everything around her an additional layer.

Gran had lived in the same house for many years.

Now generally speaking when a person lives at the same place for a period of time they create friendships with those they associate with, but not Gran.

According to her the woman who lived next door, Mrs. Smalley, who by appearance seemed of similar age was, "Nothing more than an old sticky beaking bitch." While Mr. Saunders who ran the local corner store was, "About as interesting as the soles on her shoes, with no personality at all."

Sitting quietly, I would listen as she complained to my parents how in her words, "The wind blew up his arse and his tongue waggled but nothing ever made any bloody sense."

Gran spared no one. Even Mr. Saunders shy but friendly girlfriend, Natalie was colourfully described as, "His moll that only ever seemed to be interested in sex and rooting all the time…Nothing but whore."

On every visit, Gran dominated the conversation. Yapping like a bloody fox terrier, sometimes I wondered if anyone would stand up to her and tell her to shut her bloody cake hole as she did not know everything and was far from perfect. She was so self absorbed, always steering the conversation around back to herself, her health, her bowel movements, haemorrhoids and her constant itching that could have been solved by a good hot bath. I was not sure where her lack of hygiene had originated but it was clear she only washed sparingly given the stench that emanated from her body. Not to mention her stain covered clothes that I was sure would have the ability to walk all by themselves had she bothered to remove them. Even her hands appeared dirty and rough, like brushed potatoes. They made my stomach turn especially when she reached into her biscuit barrel to retrieve biscuits she offered with her cups of tea presented in stained and chipped cups placed upon equally disgusting saucers. But in her house no one dared to argue, she ruled the roost, she could be as outspoken as she liked; she could demand what she liked, when she liked. Her attitude was enough to make even a saint swear or at the very least turn to drink. Maybe this was the reason our visits were so seldom and short. And maybe it was her attitude of superiority while in her collapsing home and this feeling of being so high and mighty that reduced the instances where she would justify leaving. Our world was an ever changing place that could be extremely overwhelming and confronting, her home albeit collapsing was her castle and she was safe there.

All I thought was, *Thank God she lives so far away.*

Branching down from Grandma Edna was my father of course and his two sisters. Aunt Margaret, she was the eldest of the siblings and Aunt Kate the youngest, in fact she was much younger only about twelve years my senior and appeared from all reports to have been a mistake.

Aunt Margaret was married to Uncle Tom, their relationship closely resembled that of my parents for he was the worker and she was the dutiful housewife. Looking at her I would describe her as a well pressed woman, her clothes always spotlessly clean and crisply ironed, make-up always applied tastefully and not a hair out of place on her head. Whenever you saw Aunt Margaret she would be talking about recipes, the desserts and cakes she had baked or the flowers she had blooming in her garden. She was not only a sweet toothed dutiful housewife but also a proud one at that.

Uncle Tom was a tall, thin and balding man of pale

complexion who did not say much at all. He was a crap collector or officially referred to as a "night carter" one of those men who used to ride around the streets on his horse and cart collecting the cans from dunnies. Maybe, I thought, that was the reason he was so quiet, maybe he was ashamed of his job or maybe it was just that with Aunt Margaret he could never manage to get a word in edgeways. To look at him at a social event you would never have imagined what a stinking job he had, for there was no stench seeping from body and his clothes like Aunt Margaret's were always in pristine condition. The only thing was with him being so tall his pant legs always ended well above his ankles making it look as if he were expecting some sort of flood. While people appreciated the job these "night carters" did many complained about the noise they made in the early hour collections referring to them as the noisy bastards. Every week the same old routine, dogs got tied up the night before then any time just after midnight you could hear the dogs barking and faint banging and crashing getting louder as they approached the neighbourhood. The final disturbance would be the sound of them running up the side of your house, the rattle of the lid clanging with every move the carters made.

Aunt Margaret and Aunt Kate were like chalk and cheese, some where along the line Aunt Kate had inherited fun genes. To her life was one big adventure, it was something you grabbed a hold of with both hands. Even the clothes she wore exude life, for many in those days chose dull tones, but not Aunt Kate. When the fashion world changed so did Kate along with her hairstyles. She was not shy to come forward with ideas nor would she shy away from expressing who she was and what she wanted. I think that is probably part of the reason why she was so successful. The hardest part of being successful is having the courage to take a chance. For Kate, nothing ever appeared too hard. One word that summed her up in a nutshell would be charismatic.

As for my great uncle, Fred, no one knew his fate after he severed all ties with his family. Defying my great grandfathers instruction to stay in Australia, he boarded a ship bound for England soon after he turned twenty-one. Gran said it was his way of escaping her father's rule. She said how her father refused to see him off stating he had betrayed his efforts, claiming to watch him board a ship headed for London would be like watching him being placed into the ground. To my great grandfather, the ship would be his coffin.

On my mother's side, there was no family history. Well, nothing that we were aware of. Mum had been left on the doorsteps of an orphanage when she was just a baby. No explanation, no clues as to her mother, just her wrapped in a blanket and placed into a carry basket.

I sometimes wondered what was worse, a history of dysfunctional relatives or no family history at all.

Unlike my ancestors, Bugsy's dated back to five generations to the first fleet where they had arrived as convicts. Life was much tougher then; his family tales spoke of struggles, hardship and perseverance in this harsh new land.

They spoke of that first voyage, which had taken eight months, of the sick and dying, the malnourished, those effected by dysentery and scurvy who never made it to Australia. A convict had a one in six chance of dying of cholera, typhoid or influenza. They were kept below the decks in dark and cramped conditions. A man of average height could not stand up right and while air pipes had been installed to improve ventilation the atmosphere was described as stifling and foul smelling. Seasickness was common and the smell of vomit, urine and sweat was only made worse when all the hatches were closed.

They also spoke of how when the first ships finally arrived every soldier and sailor, every convict and carpenter was put to work clearing away undergrowth and smaller trees putting up tents on whatever level ground they could find. Male convicts were released from the ships first and ten days later the woman disembarked. They were not told why this system was chosen. They only presumed it was to allow time for the harder jobs to be completed with less distraction. Anyhow regardless as to the reason, orders were to be followed and few dared to neither question nor argue.

Captain Arthur Phillip, who was in command and who would later become the first Governor of New South Wales had a folding canvas house, which was erected on the East side of Sydney Cove. While some of the convicts camped in this area, most were relegated to the West side above the rocks. Officers pitched tents, whilst convicts made shelters of bark, clay, twigs and branches. Unloading the ships took two days, shelters were put up for the animals they had brought, stores were unloaded and placed in mounds, sentries were posted to guard these mounds and to ensure convicts did not escape at night.

White civilisation had arrived in Australia and from across the water local Aboriginals watched and wondered. It was a new and frightening world.

Convicts worked every weekday, from sunrise to sunset, on Saturday work stopped at midday when convicts were able to wash clothes and rest. No one worked on Sunday, this was a day of rest and church services were held. Initially, months passed with no contact from the outside world, food was the most precious resource for without it everyone would die. On the cliffs of South Head a lookout was posted with instructions to raise a flag when a ship became visible on the horizon, but no ship appeared. Weekly rations were cut, then cut again, convicts dropped dead from hunger and everyone feared that if a ship did not arrive soon they would all starve. All the settlements cattle disappeared having wandered away into the bush while crops withered under the blazing sun. Sharpshooters sent out by the governor to shoot wild animals or catch fish returned with very little. Things were looking extremely grim for everyone.

Many convicts had described the conditions as intolerable and deplorable, a perfect misery. Discipline was harsh and often arbitrary. Further offences committed in the colony resulted in a variety of brutal punishments. Fifty lashes was a common punishment, this was enough to strip the skin from a mans back, it caused extreme pain, blood loss and if the individual receiving the punishment survived they would carry permanent scarring. Crews while on ships and crowds including convicts while on land were mustered to witness punishments. The whipping and cracking sound of the lashes would accompany the cries of the poor soul on the receiving end, chunks of flesh flew from his back hitting the ground, where waiting ants gathered for a feeding frenzy. Others were subject to cruelties such as wearing leg irons and working on chain gangs. These convicts were employed in the back breaking work of making new roads, stone cutting and other heavy jobs whilst wearing shackles on each ankle linked by chain that tied up to the waist to keep it out of the way. Over time, these metal shackles wore into the ankles tearing the skin.

The vast emptiness of the Australian bush, fear of being killed by Aboriginals and the fear of starvation for those first convicts was very real.

Finally, on 3rd June 1790, the flag was seen fluttering, a ship was coming and the convicts ran about hugging each other with excitement. They had not been forgotten and more ships would soon arrive bringing with them the much needed supplies.

Stories also recalled events about daring escapes, how the headline of a Sydney newspaper in June 1803 was titled "Fatal attempt to escape to China." In this instance a party of four escapees set out to walk to China having heard it was somewhere North of Sydney. Only one person survived this escape and returned. Others believed China lay beyond the Blue Mountains and many escaped convicts died while trying to walk there. All in all most of the convicts who tried to escape starved to death, were killed by the Aboriginals or gave themselves up. Still for many male convicts, escaping into the bush continued to be a possibility, a possibility that rarely resulted in freedom.

Like many that arrived as convicts, the crimes they committed were small in comparison to the punishment received. Bugsy's relative colourfully referred to as "Dicky" had been sentenced to seven years of hard labour for stealing a loaf of bread. Others sentenced for the same period also stole what could be considered as basic necessities; trousers, a shirt, a hat, a coat, a pair of boots.

By the time Dicky arrived in Sydney, he had already served two years of his sentence. What he saw before him were endless possibilities of a new life, he was not interested in joining any escape or returning to England once his sentence had been served. To him, Australia was the gateway to a new life; there was nothing he could do to change the past, for no one can change the past. He was in the present and so he had to focus on surviving the present whilst working towards a brighter future.

Dicky spoke of how he observed the behaviour of his fellow convicts and knew those who behaved well, kept a still tongue in their head and worked hard suffered less. In the end, his efforts paid off with his assignment to work for a free settler. No longer, a member of a government work gang constructing roads and government buildings. Dicky was assigned to a good master, working the same, as he would have had he remained in England. Stories spread of convicts assigned to employers who treated them cruelly, overworking them and keeping them short of food and clothes. Dicky was lucky, his employer was fair obeying all the rules regarding the hours to be worked, living conditions and the amount food and clothing rations.

And so life continued, following his head down bum up strategy Dicky worked for his employer as instructed while in his spare time tended his own vegetable garden which supplied additional nutrients required to keep him both strong and healthy.

After serving five years of his sentence, he then applied for a ticket of leave, which allowed him to work for wages in his spare time. He was two years away from total freedom, two years away from being granted a pardon at which time he would be allowed to own his own property.

To his family, Dicky was regarded as somewhat of a hero, his hard work and determination had paved the way for future generations. Whilst it was desperation and the struggle to survive that had resulted with Dicky turning to crime, understanding the pressure placed upon so many in those dreadful times meant his crime could be forgiven. Above all else, what could never be forgotten was the path Dicky took upon arriving to Australia, a path that was destined to change the fate of all future generations. For it was his actions all those years ago that had altered the Smith family forever, severing the close English ancestry ties and forging ahead with the creation of a new Australian pride.

The Smith family knew the harsh Australian climate well. Over time, they had handed down farming knowledge. They were proud of their heritage. They paid honour to Dicky and his achievements as though he were a gallant knight who had survived a great war, grateful for his tenacity and dreams of a better life. A pride emulated in their love and respect for the land. They were proud of their heritage and proud to be Australians.

CHAPTER THREE

I first met Bugsy and the Smith family when I was nine back in 1933. He was twelve although he would not admit it, to the world he was nearly thirteen - a teenager, no longer a child.

My parents had decided it was time to escape the hustle and bustle of the big smoke - Sydney. My father had heard of Dunberry from a co-worker who had visited there the year before. Apparently, it was renowned for its annual goat races. People would travel from near and far for one weekend packed full of excitement. It was the first time we had really ventured out into the country and I was in total amazement the whole way to Dunberry. My parents were surprised; not a peep was heard from the back seat. No - I need to go to the bathroom, no - I am hungry, no - I am bored and no - whining questions about how much further. The countryside was beautiful, never before had I seen so much grass, so many trees and most of all never before had I seen wild kangaroos. At one stage we stopped quite abruptly smack bang in the centre of the road, for before us was a lizard sunning itself in the middle of the road.

"Stop, stop!" my mother yelled, with a panic in her voice I had never heard before. I was sure for a split second we were going to career off the road and down the grassy embankment, which separated us from the road and fields that ran beside.

"It's a lizard," my mother exclaimed once the car stood motionless its motor humming, "A frilled-neck lizard, quick Shirley, quick lets get out of the car and have us a closer look." My eyes nearly bulged out of their sockets; at least they felt that way. From the back seat of the car, I could not see a lizard, only miles of road still to be travelled. My father, at the wheel in front of me shaking his head, he was speechless, I am sure he jumped in his seat as my mothers yell shot out of her mouth. And now, he sat still, obviously relieved her yell was not for something more serious.I had never seen a frilled- neck lizard before and was not really sure if I dared to venture from the safety of the car seat to see my first.

The next thing I knew was the door on my right opened and in grabbed my mother tugging at my arm.

"Quick or we may miss him!"

Quick, I thought, *Oh please let us be too slow, let the lizard be gone.*

However, it was not, and to my surprise, it was not as frightening as I had first imagined. With all the commotion my mother had made I thought I was about to be introduced to a version of an extinct dinosaur. The poor little lizard still sunning itself in the centre of the road oblivious to the excitement around. After a few closer looks and pokes with a stick, so as to see the frill around its neck my mother told me it was time to save him as she gently pushed him to the side of the road. Making our way back to the car, I was both excited and relieved at my discovery. The image of the poor defenceless lizard took a place in my mind as we were again back on the road.

It is only now as I write I realise how many small factors of my childhood I actually remember. You could ask me what I did yesterday and sometimes I would probably find it difficult to tell. I guess we all have days like those. These days you don't see as many lizards on the road, not frilled-necks, for that matter if you do see them they are generally flat as a tack.

During our trip to Dunberry in 1933, I can only recall seeing a car every so often. Where as now if you were to take the same trip I would imagine it would be difficult to lose sight of all vehicles.

By the time we made it to Dunberry, I was exhausted. During the trip, I had nodded off several times. Sitting in the back seat the sun found rest on the left side of my face and neck, the effects of which I felt as the cool night air rolled in over the hills.

That night we took up lodgings at The Royal Hotel, Dunberry's local pub. Although I had not exerted much energy physically throughout our journey my body felt drained. All the new discoveries, my thoughts and the constant studying of our wondrous countryside had left me mentally exhausted. During dinner, I battled with my tiredness, straining to keep my eyes open, constantly yawning until finally I conceded defeat and said my goodnights. It was an early night for me, what adventures lay before us, I could only dream about.

And oh did I dream that night. It's funny that people can dream so much. They say that dreams are the mysterious language of the night, distant hopes or ideals, idle thoughts. Studies show, that the average person will reportedly experience four to five dreams during a night. In fact, it is believed each of us spends approximately twenty per cent of our total sleep time or one and a half hours per night dreaming, yet, generally as soon as we wake the dream is gone. As we lay in bed, we know that we have experienced a dream yet the exact details are amiss.

I remembered some of the details from one of my dreams that night I was surrounded by talking kangaroos, koalas, emus, wombats, possums and frilled-neck lizards. They spoke to me of the natural beauty I would soon discover. They were all so friendly and as inquisitive of me as I was of them. Climbing on the back of one of the kangaroos I was taken on a tour of the flower filled hills and drank at the crystal clear water holes they explained were home to so many.

They spoke of the natural beauty our country had to offer, of how this beauty should always be protected for once it was gone it may never return. Lying amongst the native flowers, I listened to the animals and the birds in the surrounding trees until finally I closed my eyes. I was at peace with the land and its wild creatures.

CHAPTER FOUR

1933 was also the year Hitler came to power and by now the effects of the Great Depression were being felt all around the world. It appeared the halcyon days were over for many.

I did not realise then what an impact the holiday at Dunberry would have on the rest of my life. Had I realised then, well, maybe I would have done things differently. Isn't that what we all think when we sit down and reflect on our lives. What if…what if I had done that or what if I hadn't done that? I guess we should not worry about the what ifs in the world but as humans I don't think that is possible. Always analysing different scenarios, why a simple task can take twice as long to complete, sometimes even longer, with most of the time taken by a close analysis. What if I do it that way or what if I do it this way?

Sometimes when I was growing up, my mother would nag at my father, trying to get things around the house completed. I remember when it was time for him to lop the large gum tree in our backyard; it took him over two months just to get the job started. Mum constantly reminded him and his reply would always be that he was analysing the situation properly so that he would cause no damage to the house or items close by should a branch fall incorrectly. Somehow, I don't think he spent much time analysing the what if scenarios, more so it was procrastination. My father, although at times unbearably strict, had a very laid back attitude and an even greater fear of heights; this did not help his motivation towards the tree lopping exercise. However, when he eventually summoned enough courage he nearly took down the whole tree; there would be no need of lopping for years to come.

Back to 1933 and my first encounter with William "Bugsy" Smith, from which I seem to have digressed. It was the first morning of our stay at Dunberry; I woke early having gone to bed just after eight the previous night. As I mentioned before, we stayed at The Royal Hotel although this was to be a camping holiday. My parents were also too tired to bother with anything and had opted to take an easy option for the first night.

It was just before six-thirty and the sun was coming up over the horizon, its rays penetrating the fog that had rolled in over the farmlands scattered as far as the eye could see. There was a crispness to the morning air, a freshness I had never experienced. As I exhaled clouds of breath left my mouth, my hands tucked into my purple woollen jumper, which I had slipped on for extra warmth its arms stretched out of shape. My nightie felt as though it had turned to ice, so I stood still trying to keep the loose fabric from touching my legs. I was lucky, there wasn't much of a breeze just a crisp freshness surrounding me. A countryside coming to life by the morning sun, which at that early hour carried no warmth only light. I was standing on the verandah of our hotel room; the street below was still quiet. In the distance, I could hear the noise of local farmers completing their morning tasks of feeding and milking the cattle.

In the quiet street below, I noticed a figure walking towards the hotel. Not an adult, the figure was too small to belong to an adult. I stood still watching, it was carrying what appeared to be a basket, of what I did not know. As the figure got closer I could tell it belonged to a boy, probably around my age or maybe a little older, he was wearing trousers, with a patch on the right knee, held up by braces. By this time I could also see the basket, inside were eggs. My mind wandered, *yummy* I thought, *fresh eggs*. My stomach started to growl as I thought of scrambled eggs on toast and maybe some fresh crispy bacon. I closed my eyes and inhaled deeply, trying to smell what my stomach desired.

"What ya doin' up there?" came a voice from below, my eyes sprang open. The smell of my imaginary breakfast was gone in a flash.

"What ya doin' up there, Red?"

It was the boy below; he was obviously talking to me calling me "Red" in reference to the red ringlets I possessed.

"What ya looking so strangely for?" he continued.

To which I quickly responded, "I am not looking strangely, you are the strange one."

Oh no! I thought, had that last response really come out of my mouth or had I just thought it?

I heard a chuckle of laughter below followed by another remark.

"Ya not from round ere are ya, little girl?"

I felt heat rise in my face and it was not from the rising sun. *Little girl! Whom did he think he was talking to?*

"Sticks and stones will break my bones but names will never hurt me," a response typical of a nine year old rolled from my lips. I thought now he will really think I am a little girl.

"Bugsy, that's what thems call me round ere."

"Shirley, Shirley Rumming," I replied.

"No, I am from Sydney visiting on two weeks holidays with my folks."

He did not seem at all concerned with my previous childish response more so interested in finding out who I was and where I was from. After a brief exchange of pleasantries, Bugsy bid me farewell assuring me that we would meet again.

And that, was my first encounter.

After watching him disappear under the verandah I stood upon I decided it was time to head back into the warmth of our room and wait until my parents woke. My family and I spent the rest of our two week holiday camped by the local, Stiles River. Bugsy became the daily visitor. My father referred to him as a pleasant lad, while my mother voiced no opinion, appearing only to be happy I had made a new friend.

Setting up camp was a near painful experience for me, never in my life had I had to pitch a tent. Canvas, ropes and tent pegs were scattered before me like pieces of an impossible jigsaw puzzle. Echoes of wild birds squawking and chirping surrounded us. Besides those and the commands my father was issuing, everything appeared so peaceful, so still, so serene. It was amazing. Looking across the river into the bush, I could only try to imagine what it would have been like for the first explorers who set foot here. I was sure they would have questioned what creatures' lay beneath the water, what they would next discover when climbing over the rock faces on the other side of the river. Rock faces, which extended to great heights blocking further views of the great new land. This place was amazing and I was sure, I was going to experience a holiday like no other.

Just in case you were wondering, yes I did have

scrambled eggs on that first morning, fresh farm eggs lightly beaten, with creamy milk straight from the cows and a sprinkle of parsley straight out of the garden. Never before had my taste buds experienced such wonder. The toast, ah, the toast, that too was freshly baked, topped with lashings of whipped butter. There were no artificial additives or genetics involved in this breakfast, just fresh produce and some early morning risers to combine all the natural ingredients. Bugsy delivered the fresh farm eggs daily as a part of his chores and they were enjoyed by many of the Hotel patrons who selected from the Hotel's blackboard menu of culinary delights.

Once our campsite was established, it didn't take long for Bugsy to stumble upon us, after all Dunberry wasn't a large place and it appeared everyone knew everyone's business and everything that happened. Especially, when it involved the whereabouts of strangers within there midst. Formally introducing himself to my parents and I Bugsy gave us a quick run down on the area, its history and also offered his assistance if required. Bugsy then offered to give me a guided tour of the surroundings. Looking towards my father for permission, he acknowledged the offer with a nod of his head. Bugsy's uniqueness intrigued me and I was elated by my father's decision.

Leaving our campsite, we followed the natural flow of the river until we came across a small trail, which branched out, to the left. Pausing for a moment, Bugsy explained it led to his family property. He first stumbled across our camp down this trail that he had ventured. It was also the trail that he took when going fishing, when embarking on expeditions to the local caves or taking a short cut to neighbouring properties.

By the time my holidays were over, I would become familiar with every dip, rock and overhanging branch along this trail. Leading on, Bugsy instructed me to place my feet where his had left the ground. Setting a steady pace, he guided me up the windy trail at times surrounded by long grass, ducking and weaving between branches. Finally, after carefully manoeuvring our way along slippery slopes we clambered over a rock outcrop and reached a gathering of trees beyond which stood Bugsy's house.

Making our way across the front yard towards the porch of the house Bugsy pointed in the direction of a barn located on our right. I had noticed this aging structure on our approach and as my eyes followed the course of Bugsy's finger. I questioned the relevance of his pointing.

"What?" I questioned shrugging my shoulders.

"There's my dad!" Bugsy proclaimed proudly.

Tractors, an old horse cart, stacks of sheet metal, old wheel axles and many items that appeared to be nothing more than junk decorated the barn surrounds. Then from behind a large stack of wood emerged a man wearing a torn green sweater, holey overalls and black gumboots. Totally oblivious to our presence he was hard at work swinging an axe, chopping and stacking wood. Looking back towards Bugsy I smiled and nodded.

"Come on, let me introduce you to my mum," he summonsed me to follow on.

Sweet smelling, tantalising and mouth watering aromas danced up the hallway escaping through the front door and out onto the porch greeting us. I was relieved, I had made it there in one piece. As we made our way inside these aromas intensified and so we followed our noses until we made it to the kitchen where ingredients, mixing bowls, cooking utensils and freshly baked goods covered the benches. Bugsy introduced me to his mother Beatrice, a petite woman who possessed a very endearing and welcoming smile. Offering me a glass of water and place to sit she instructed Bugsy to summons his father for some well deserved afternoon tea.

Sitting at the kitchen table with Bugsy each of us sipping a glass of water, I heard the front door slam and in emerged Jack, Bugsy's father. Immediately, Bugsy rose to his feet and introduced me. Jack wiping his dusty hand down the side of his overalls then extended his hand shaking mine and welcomed me to his home.

Together, the four of us sat around the kitchen table, exchanging pleasantries and details about who we were and where we were from. Jack was a countryman through and through, his face while rough from years under the harsh sun also radiated a caring personality.

A farmers life was tough, full of early mornings, demanding chores and unforeseen challenges. Jack knew nothing else than how to work the land; the seasons, demands and gruelling deadlines dominated his life. Deadlines associated by the cattle they had to look after and the crops, which required sowing and harvesting no matter what hand, the weather dealt.

As a farmer to be successful, you required a passion for all the land represented, a drive to keep going no matter what and a hope and belief that at the end of the day everything would be all right. Everything would work out for the best and be as it was supposed to be. Jack appeared to possess a natural wisdom and said things exactly as he saw them. Although I considered my father to be a wise man, this was a different wisdom. It was not obtained through reading books; life and all it offered imparted this wisdom.

Outside, the sun was beginning to set, so I bid my farewells. Bugsy guided me back to our campsite with the promise of more adventures.

The following morning, at about seven o'clock and for every other morning of our holidays Bugsy would greet us with half a dozen eggs still sitting in his basket and a great big, "Mornin' all, Mornin' Red." Together we would sit by the campfire, eat our breakfast, Bugsy's second and plan our adventures for the day. During that holiday, I think I would have done more walking than I had ever done in my life. We walked along the river, along the creek, went for swims in the water holes and the dam which was on Bugsy's farm. We climbed trees and into caves, over rocky outcrops, rode horses, chased the sheep through the fields and I even shared my first kiss, with Bugsy. Unlike him, I had never had a nickname and I welcomed my affectionately created title of "Red," I felt special.

Bugsy and I never argued at all, oh, except about Bugsy's age, which he continually insisted he was a teenager. It seemed as if we were made for each other, like we were two hands belonging to the same body with one mind. We enjoyed the same things, even food. Both of us said we gagged at the thought of eating mushrooms and spinach, yet, did not mind anything else. Peas and carrots is how Bugsy would describe us, "Like peas and carrots…We go together."

Bugsy would act a clown sometimes and show off, I remember one time when he was showing off he decided to jump on the back of a ram they owned. The ram was rather large and had long horns protruding from its head; Bugsy climbed on saying that he was a cowboy. Before he knew it the ram was bucking and running all around the paddock, Bugsy's arms flew up in the air and the ram bucked him off into the blackberry bushes. I laughed so hard that I feared I might wet myself. Bruised and battered Bugsy rose to his feet, not admitting he had hurt himself, dusted himself off and yelled, "Wow, what a ride!" Then he limped around for days.

Bugsy also claimed to be a champion climber. Gathering ropes, he found in the barn, he decided that he would show me how to climb to the top of the barn. Everything went as planned on his climb to the top. However, when he made it up there, coming down was a different story.My feet remained firmly on the ground even with him insisting that it would be safe. Distracted by his dog Bandit barking I looked away from Bugsy's direction returning my attention when I heard a cracking sound. Bugsy was gone. At first, I thought he had crawled down the slope of the other side, although I soon discovered him lying on the pile of hay inside the barn. Some of the shingles on the roof had given way and for Bugsy, it was an unexpected trip straight down. Again, he was left bruised and battered, but he did not admit that he hurt himself. With all the skylarking he did I was amazed he did not injure himself more severely. He was definitely braver than I was, fear was not a part of his make up.

While my time was taken up with exploring and adventures, my father took on the role of hunter and gatherer. Packed within our luggage was a selection of fishing rods and traps. After talking to some of his work mates he decided he would test his hand at rabbiting and fishing. Although his first attempts did not prove fruitful, persistence paid off and I could see how proud he was of his achievements as he boasted about his catches of the day. Also packed within our luggage were my mothers sewing boxes. Along with preparing our meals and doing the washing daily, my mother filled her time with sewing, knitting and reading.

At night, we would sit by the camp fire and exchange stories. Occasionally, Bugsy would also join us for dinner, supplying us with meat and fresh vegetables from his parents' farm. I do not recall my family ever talking as much as we did over our campfire at Dunberry. Don't get me wrong, we did communicate but we just never seemed to sit down and talk or listen to each other at all, other than when we were at Dunberry around the campfire. That puzzles me, for the life of me I don't know why.

The day we left Dunberry was a sad occasion; Bugsy came around in the morning as he had done every morning before. However, this time there was no excitement in our conversation, no plans for new adventures. It was time for me to leave this wonderful place, time to head back to the hustle and bustle of the big smoke.

Behind me I would leave Bugsy, wondering what it was like to see the Harbour Bridge, its construction now completed and officially opened in 1932, to see the beautiful Harbour over which it crossed. I had described to him how for many years I had watched as the two halves rose separately on each side of the Harbour. The wonderful futuristic design, eventually meeting and how we had attended its opening amongst thousands of people. Cheers sweeping through the crowd. I had described to him what it was like to swim in the ocean.

To feel the salt spray as the waves came crashing around you - all these things I took for granted, all these things he was yet to experience. It's amazing how we do take things for granted, how we don't realise that many others, probably millions of other people would love to experience even just part of what we experience. I had never really thought about things like that until I saw the expression on Bugsy's face when I first described the rolling waves of the ocean.

We exchanged addresses and promised to write to each other, Bugsy promised to tell me how many puppies his pregnant collie Bandit had. He promised he would name one after me.

"Paddy, short for Paddington where you live, that's what I will call it, then I will never forget where you live."

He sounded so sincere, I knew without a doubt he would name one of the pups Paddy.

CHAPTER FIVE

The saying how time flies when you are having fun, is said to be so true, but let me tell you time also flies when not is all just fun. Sitting here writing my tale, I am far from that sweet nine-year-old who sat in the back seat of her parents' car. The one who sat still her eyes nearly popping out of their sockets, fearing a frilled-neck lizard may resemble an extinct dinosaur she had studied at school. More than sixty-five years have past since that day and if you asked me would I do it all again, the answer would definitely be a big fat NO.

We arrived back in Paddington on a Saturday afternoon. My mother, in all her wisdom had agreed with my father that returning on Saturday would be best. We would all be able to have a good nights sleep then on Sunday she could complete all the washing and household chores prior to the new working week and school.

Sunday night dinners were always something light and easy, with the main meal of the week being our Sunday lunch. This lunch usually consisted of roasted lamb or beef, potatoes and two other vegetables covered in lashings of gravy followed by a homemade apple pie or pudding. Dinner on the other hand was usually PMU baked beans or spaghetti on toast, soup or leftovers from lunch all chopped up and fried together called bubble and squeak.

On the Sunday night of our return, we had scrambled eggs on toast; they were fresh eggs Bugsy had given us on our departure, yet the eggs never tasted as they had back in Dunberry.

After dinner my mother cleared away the plates, washed the dishes and prepared my fathers lunch. Two jam sandwiches and a large piece of cake.Always the same, not only was my father one who had a laidback attitude he also had no imagination. Porridge followed by sausages, eggs and toast for breakfast, jam sandwiches always for lunch then meat, potatoes and two vegetables for dinner excluding Sunday nights. I was sure, if they ever stopped making jam my father would think the end of the world was near.

Dad was the working man, the man of the house, and the breadwinner. That was the way most families ran in those days. My mother served my father, one fixed point in a changing age. The wife's place was at home in the kitchen and taking care of the children while the husband went to work and provided for his family - how things have changed.

Our methodicalness also returned when we arrived back in Paddington. It was as if a greater force controlled us all. I was sure my parents had spies to watch my every move, ensuring I lived my life in accordance with the rules they had set that would ensure all required tasks were accomplished. My time in Dunberry, although brief, was a stark contrast to that in Paddington.

With my parents, I was made to sit and eat food I did not like. To complain about a meal would demonstrate ungratefulness and an ungrateful child would be punished. Disrespectful attitudes would not be tolerated, no matter how small the instruction and so I would grudgingly adhere to their demands. Things like washing my hands and keeping my nails clean seemed like small issues but they represented so much more. I was a child when I was allowed to be, although I had to grow up fast. My father wanted discipline and respect.

After dinner, I helped with drying the dishes, before I was allowed outside to play on my scooter. Once outside, I scanned the street looking for other children I could play with. Petra was up the street with her neighbour Sarah, who I did not really know, they were playing hopscotch so I jumped on my scooter and rode up there to join in. It was not before too long that other children came to join in our games. We all stood around chatting away telling tales of our holiday adventures. Billy, who lived in the next street came around, on his initial approach I noticed he had a slingshot in his hand. However, as he got closer he slid it into his back pocket so as no one would see. Billy was renowned for causing trouble and it was not too long before trouble followed him. Listening to our stories it was clear, he was either bored or jealous as he made interrupting remarks and silly noises. Taking the slingshot from his pocket he reached to the ground and picked up a rock pulled back on the band and sent the rock flying through grumpy Mrs. Sharp's window. The window smashed on impact and us kids were out of there in a flash. I flew back down the street on my scooter, not looking back to see what happened next.

I wonder what ever happened to Billy, as we grew older his escapades, became more daring and dangerous. At one stage, I heard he had been involved in an armed robbery. This did not surprise me. In fact, I would not be at all surprised if Billy had murdered someone in his time; he had a violent streak that you did not want to cross even at that young age. He would boast how he would kill birds with his sling shot or sit still waiting for a stray cat to shoot at or take to the water and drown. He made my skin crawl and every attempt was made to keep a safe distance between us.

After the incident on the street with the window, I decided it would be safer to remain at home. I did not want to be involved in the questioning. I did not want to point the finger at Billy and so I retreated to my bedroom. Downstairs, I could hear music playing and my parents talking. I showered, put on my nightie, said my good nights and went to bed. Tomorrow it was back to school, back to reality.

That night I had a nightmare, in which bad boy Billy waved his slingshot in the air. His hands were covered in blood. We were standing in the street and laughter echoed around us.

"I got her," he said, "I got that Mrs. Sharp, right between the eyes and she howled like a whiny cat." His laughter again echoed around me. His devil like eyes peered at me and as he grinned, vampire-like teeth protruded from his mouth.

"You're next!"

I woke shaking and in a cold sweat, my nightmare had been so lifelike. I worried about Mrs. Sharp. What if my nightmare was a warning of what was to follow? What if he had really shot Mrs. Sharp and she lay dead in a pool of blood? I had no doubt that he would be capable of such an act and I was sure he would laugh about it too. Maybe, I was to be his next victim.

Before I was able to fall back to sleep, I heard Mr. Cummings our next door neighbour leave for work; he was a baker and started his working day at three.

I had known Mr. Cummings all my life, he had always appeared extremely reserved, a man of few words. This was a stark contrast to the man my mother described him as being long before I had made my way into the world. Years before, tragedy had struck and his life had been shattered by the loss of his wife in a drowning accident on the Nepean River. The coroners' inquest revealed Catherine; his wife had taken a dip to cool both her and their baby daughter Meredith when her feet became entwined in floating debris. Witnesses stated, they heard a male's hellish scream for help before running to the river. Arriving at the scene, they saw a male waist deep in the water grabbing a baby off a young woman who was also screaming for help before she was dragged beneath the water surface. All attempts to save the woman including lassoing the debris failed and although what they witnessed appeared to be happening in slow motion many believed the victim vanished in a matter of seconds. The baby was rescued unscathed but screaming. In that instant, Mr. Cummings had been propelled into a new life, that of a widower and single parent. He had adored his wife, they had been childhood sweethearts. My mother said he worshipped the ground she walked on, proudly declaring his love for her to all he met, she was his soul mate and with her he said life was complete.

Word quickly spread of his loss, offers of support, messages of condolences came flooding in but it appeared all too much and so he withdrew from all social activity. From that day on, his one and only focus became his daughter, Meredith. As the years rolled by Mr. Cummings withdrawal continued. His face told the story of heartache and sorrow. Meredith blossomed into a fine young woman.

Although Meredith's role within my life was that of

a babysitter, she became to mean so much more. For she was one of the most honest, thoughtful, kind and caring people, I had ever had the pleasure of knowing. Like the big sister I never had, Meredith was both protective and fun to be around and I loved her.

Sadly for me, Meredith left home around the time I commenced school. Her dream in life was to visit America and it was a dream she had accomplished. Not only did she visit there, she stayed there and with her new family, she lived in a town called Tishomingo in Mississippi.

So now, it was just Mr. Cummings and his cat, Goldie. As Mr. Cummings closed his front door, I heard him talk to Goldie. In his voice I could hear no fear and I found comfort in the fact his cat was safe and well.

My bedroom was filled with the light from the lamppost out front. In the gentle breeze, the shadows cast from branches of the trees outside appeared as outstretched arms embracing my room. I lay in my bed watching the arms as they wandered all over my floor, the walls and me. I thought of the fun times Meredith and I had shared and let out a sigh as I recalled the love I felt when she embraced me in her arms.

Bad boy Billy was not nearby, he was probably tucked up in his own bed. I assured myself that it had just been a silly nightmare and I closed my eyes as I snuggled beneath my blankets. Feeling the fibres of my sheets as I gently rubbed them between my fingers, I continued to reassure myself. I was safe.

CHAPTER SIX

For weeks after our arrival back in Paddington, I would rush down to our letterbox waiting for news from Bugsy. The Postman used to deliver twice daily and on Saturdays back then. At last, after three weeks the letter arrived, I knew straight away, its envelope displayed the word "Red" where normally my parents names would be written. I sat on the footpath engrossed in every word. Bandit had her litter only two days after we left; five healthy pups, one named Paddy.

Bugsy's words recalled our adventures and events, which had happened since our leaving Dunberry, three pages in all.At the bottom, he signed off with, "Your friend always." I sat there holding the letter to my chest; he was different from anyone else I had ever met. Life and energy appeared to seep from his every pore.

The holidays were over and I had returned to school, telling tales of my adventures as many sat around mouths wide open, listening to every detail. I did not have to invent or exaggerate any of my experiences to attract interest, as for many in the city these experiences were exciting just as they had happened. I was the envy of all. Collecting horse dung and selling it for fertiliser or feeding chickens in their backyards was the closest many had gotten to the country. Their faces displayed the same expression Bugsy's had when I had described to him the Harbour Bridge and the rolling waves of the ocean.

Two months later, I celebrated my tenth birthday and my parents put on a huge party. I was allowed to invite twelve of my friends from school. In all, including our relatives and friends of the family there were over thirty people. During the celebration we feasted on all types of treats; fairy bread, little frankfurts, mini pies, angel cakes and sweets all wonderfully prepared by my mother. We even had Peters ice cream with Milo sprinkled all over it for pudding. There were many different games, among them bobbing for apples, marbles, hide and seek and musical chairs.

Finally, at the very end of the day, all of the lights were turned off and out of the kitchen emerged my mother carrying my birthday cake. Ten candles on top all flickering away as the guests broke into Happy Birthday. It was the perfect end, to a wonderful day. My school friends each left with a lollie bag and a piece of birthday cake.

I was the centre of attention when I went to school the next Monday, again the envy of so many. In those days, so many families found it difficult to afford the basics in life. I had had a party that vast numbers could only dream about.

I enjoyed my school years. At the time, I was in primary school and my teacher was Sally Lincoln, she was fair but very strict, as were most of the teachers. However, I was a good pupil, one who completed my homework and always sat up straight at my desk. I was a star pupil and in Mrs. Lincoln's eyes, I could do no wrong. Being one of her favourites, I was awarded the job of "Ink Monitor." It was a good job where I would have to mix up the ink. Retrieving a big bottle of powder I would add water, give it a stir then distribute the ink into the ink wells on our desks paying particular attention to ensure I did not spill a drop.

School was very different in those days. For all students focus was placed heavily upon reading, writing and arithmetic. As soon as you entered, primary school boys and girls were desegregated. It was all quite divorced, even playtime time, all of us housed within a common school grounds the boys now attending Technical School on one side with subjects like drawing classes, science, woodwork and metalwork. While us, girls attended Home Science School with subjects that included home training, gymnastics, cooking and needlework.

Each morning when the school bell rang muster would be called where we would line up at attention singing, "God save the King"; all students in class rows like regimented soldiers. The class teachers walking around ensuring everyone was standing still. In winter, we would shiver and freeze, at times you could hear teeth chattering together. While in summer, it was bloody hot standing on the asphalt. Most of us girls wore shoes and still the heat would penetrate our soles. From the boys' school, where many did not wear shoes, you would hear stories of young lads getting into trouble at muster due to moving around. I could only imagine the pain they would have endured; the asphalt was that hot at times I was sure you could have fried an egg on it. And there were the teachers yelling at them to stand still ignoring the fact that their moving was simply done in an effort to stop the burning.

When assembly was over the headmaster who ran our assembly would yell, "Attention!" followed by, "About face!" Like ants all in a row, we would perform what was demanded. We would about face and our class teacher would now be standing in front of our row. Class by class, we were dismissed and would march to our classrooms ready for a day of lessons.

Playtime would arrive at eleven o'clock, that was the time all students had to consume our dreaded quarter pint or just under two hundred millilitres of milk. Milk, that had arrived before the start of school and had been placed into the lunch shed. It was disgusting. And you had to drink it no matter how much complaining you insisted with. Just by looking at it, you could tell it had already curdled. The silver lid bulging, as if the milk was trying to escape the glass bottle. Teachers had the answers for everything. If you whined about it being lumpy, the teachers simply insisted the lumps were the creams sitting on the top.

We had some characters for teachers and many of them were given nicknames. One I had in my first year of High School, was Joe Davidson. He was the local clown, well not a clown but a real character. As soon as the bell rang, Joe would be on his bike and up to the local Murphys Pub. The only way he got home was because his bike knew the way. He was a character but a good teacher. He used to teach mathematics, algebra, trigonometry and all of that. If you were talking or you were not paying attention, he would come charging through the classroom with his broken baseball bat that had a point on it, pointing towards the culprit. Screaming as he charged up the aisle, "I'll spear you if you don't shut up!" Of course, it was all bravado he never hit anyone, but the threats were enough. His nickname was "Joedy."

Then there was Minnie Hackett, nicknamed "hatchet" due to her possessing a long, thin and unpleasant looking face with a pointed nose and chin. Her wooden ruler with its brass strip insert always accompanied her. She was my class teacher when I was in third class, before I advanced into Sally Lincoln's class. Minnie and Sally were like chalk and cheese. Minnie along with teaching a variety of subjects like Sally also taught music and we had a school choir.The music class was designed with tiered seating; I sat in the front row just near centre. She would walk up and down and around and about waving her ruler in the air demanding that we sat up straight with our feet firmly on the floor, legs together.

"I can see what you have had for breakfast!" she would yell as her ruler made contact with either her hand or a desk close by. One day while practicing our singing Minnie squawked, "Who is making that terrible noise?" and she stopped in front of me stating, "Rumming out!" That was the end of my singing career.

When the War arrived, in my later years of school many of the younger teachers who were men went into the army and schools had to call on the services of retired teachers. Now some of those were absolute gentlemen. Like my English teacher Joseph Cameron, nicknamed "Mr. Canman", who had a wonderful command for the English language. He had the ability of making student believe anything was possible, thus his nickname. He was a true gentleman, no doubt about it.

In my final year of school, my English teacher well at least for the first half of the year before he was asked to leave was old Alfred Noonan. He was afforded two nicknames, "Sparkles" and "Flapper." Mr. Noonan looked as though he was is his nineties. And I do believe his age was the reason for him leaving, although he probably was not in his nineties he would have been at least in his late seventies or early eighties. He was a sincere character, very caring and genuine. His face was lived-in and craggy, with deep lines and furrows. It looked as though he had experienced an interesting life. He would totter around wearing coke bottle glasses over his large protruding ears, squinting and smiling, nodding to acknowledge everyone in his path. He was one of the few teachers that appeared to be there due to his love of teaching. In those days, all your books were school property; you had one book called an exam book. Poor old Mr. Noonan was handing out our exam books before he departed for one last time. When he got to me, he paused and asked if he could keep mine, it was only an exam book and it did not mean anything to me so I said yes. When I looked up at him he was crying, I don't know why, I could only assume he liked my work. It was a sad day when Mr. Noonan waddled out the classroom door for that last time. His head drooped down. He was never heard from or seen by anyone ever again.

It's amazing how clearly I can remember all these names and I can't remember my own name sometimes.

All through my schooling, the dinner bell signified one hour of free time in which we could eat lunch; children bundled out into the lunch shed eating sandwiches they had packed from home. Some would go home, for it was lunchtime and you could go anywhere. Times have changed now, attitudes have changed, it would be too dangerous to do that now but back then you could disappear as long as you showed up for your next class. For some, it was a trip to the shop for a sandwich or pie or for others, it was a quick dash home, there were no provisions for meals at the school itself.

It was after I finished schooling, when the War was over, as the soldiers returned and started to come back as teachers that the real tough practices started. Some wanted to run the schools like an army camp, all regimented and no one liked it. I was relieved I had finished, as I heard stories from those younger than me who lived nearby.

Tom Lynch, now he was a real sadistic bastard, ex-army he was always giving out six of the best with his cane. Many boys fell victim to his antics. Six, quick whacks across the palm of their hands with the cane for what was referred to as insubordination. There were no laws in those days to prevent physical repercussions. Just as parents assumed the rights to chastise, strap, slap, backhand or bash their child until in some cases they were red raw or bruised, teachers had the right to inflict punishment during school hours when they deemed it necessary. All the children in the neighbourhood thought it was the greatest thing in the world when Tom Lynch blew up the science laboratory. The story went that while he was showing his students how to dilute acid instead of putting the acid into the water, he put the water into the acid and up she went. No one was hurt, there was a great cloud of smoke, everyone was evacuated but it was the funniest thing that ever happened. Everyone thought it was wonderful. Tom Lynch blew up the science laboratory.

As I say, they were very different times, as for Billy, his schooling experience was greatly different to most; from all accounts, it was also extremely challenging for both him and his teachers. Just as I was sure we would be sitting on the same hard wooden benches with their inkwells, I too was sure Billy would receive the strap or cane for his boldness and bad behaviour.

Listening to the stories, I would often sit and wonder how long it would take him to learn that at school his antics would not be tolerated. Apparently, he did not flinch when he received the strap or cane; he would stand there with a grin on his face. I could never work out if he in fact enjoyed receiving the punishment or if his grin was a sign of contempt. He did not seem to care what anyone said or what punishment he received. His mother had died when he was young and his father was an alcoholic. Billy had no rules at home and no-one not even the headmaster with his cane would make him conform.

He was the product of an environment shrouded in violence and abuse, which everyone knew, existed and no one cared or bothered to change. Unfortunately, for my friend Petra, her house backed onto his, and while most of the local houses displayed reasonably neat and tidy yards, Billy's house resembled the local garbage tip. Empty bottles, crates, rusted metal work and old discarded toys from younger years poked through overgrown lawn and bushes. In the back corner, stood an abandoned chicken coop, all its previous inhabitants had been eaten by the two family dogs who were also notorious around the neighbourhood. Their crime, repetitive nuisance and scavenging. Not that you could blame them, it would sadden and even sicken me at times to see them scanning and sniffing out for anything which would assist in their plight to survive. Their ribs and hip bones protruding, in summer their ears eaten by flies and bleeding. How the authorities failed to act and remove the dogs I will never know, in my eyes the neglect they received was along the line of cruelty. But then again, who was I to question; maybe their resources were focused on larger and more pressing matters.

Week in and week out, yelling and the sound of things being smashed could be heard from Billy's house. From Petra's, disturbances beyond the back fence appeared as a ritual. Most of the time, the yelling would commence as soon as Billy's father walked through the front door. He was drunk more often than not and always hungry when he staggered home at night. Failure to hear any disturbance would only create suspicion that something was gravely wrong. The constant repetition and abnormality of these events had over time become not only accepted as a part of life but also expected by those who lived in adjoining properties.In Petra's house, greater concern was held for Billy and his father when silence was experienced.

It was not unusual for Billy to arrive at school sporting a black eye or bruised limbs; it was not unusual for him to skip class altogether. A truant, a rebel, a survivor, maybe he could have been classified as all three. A truant is a child who idly or without excuse stays away from school. A rebel, one who resents and resists authority, refusing to conform to the generally accepted mode of behaviour. A survivor is a person who takes measures for their personal protection from attack in a struggle for existence. Billy definitely possessed these qualities and although his behaviour may not have appeared orthodox, under the circumstances maybe he was doing his best.

When his father was done with him at night, you could often hear what Billy believed was his secret sobbing. In public, he was nothing less than fearless, daring, cruel and unstoppable. I would go as far as to say he was at times evil in his actions. Maybe the dark side of Billy was a façade created as a way of helping him cope with his situation. For without these qualities, Billy would merely be seen as a scared, sobbing, cry-baby and being a cry-baby at school would only signal additional abuse and bullying from fellow students. But, with his true characteristics disguised so well, no one dared to question the tough guy with a bad attitude.

And so, life continued on, generally after school I would rush home and complete my homework before I went out to play. Children in those days were outside more so than they are today. Many of my friends were not as fortunate as I was and we would invent games of our own. All us girls would bring along our dolls, my favourite was my kewpie doll. She had big eyes, which looked straight at you and a cheeky grin. She had been a present for my fifth birthday and wherever I went my kewpie doll followed. One of the games I most enjoyed was hide and seek, we could play this for hours. When Billy joined in he would never be found. No one dared to venture into his hidey-holes.

Another game we played was, "What's the time Mr. Wolf?" One person would be the "Wolf" standing in front with their back to us while the rest of us would stand away in a line and ask what the time was. The wolf would then reply, if he/she said one o'clock we would take one pace forward, if he/she said nine o'clock we would take nine paces forward. Until the reply was, "dinnertime" at which stage we would all run off screaming and the wolf would take chase until a new wolf was caught. It was a fun game and my strategy was to take small steps therefore I would be further away and my chances of being caught were reduced.

Easter time was a fun time of the year as well. We would go on Easter egg hunts; all the kids in my street would join in. We would wake early in the morning and search for the Easter Bunny. It was great. We would follow what we believed were his trails until they seemed to disappear into thin air. One year, I think it was when

I was about eleven, Billy joined in with the trailing. We were a little sceptical about his enthusiasm at first, as he had never joined our searches previously. But on this occasion, I recalled Billy appeared unusually happy and full of cheer.

"I am on top of the world," he exclaimed as he approached.

"Why?"

"Dad spoke to me!"

"Oh, that's nice, what did he say?

"Get the fuck out of my way or I will knock your head off!" he grinned.

And with that he commenced whistling as happy as Larry, leaving us all speechless where we stood. After a moment of looking at him and still astounded by his response, I noticed that he was in fact genuinely happy and so I responded.

"That's nice Billy, I am glad you are having a nice Easter."

Exchanging smiles Billy urged, "Let the fun begin!" There were eight of us all searching together until mysteriously the track appeared to go two separate ways. Splitting into two groups, I parted Billy's company and the search continued. A few minutes later, I heard loud terrifying screams. It was Petra, she was as white as a ghost. She did not stop when she made it to us. She just kept running down the street into her house. Next thing I knew, Billy came out of the alley laughing profusely. In his hand he held a rabbit, its throat cut. Its body covered in blood. His hands covered in blood. He was sick and so was his vicious Easter prank. The group of searchers disbanded. The game was over and my parents warned me that I would be severely punished, should they ever see me in Billy's company again.

That was the last search I made trying to find the Easter Bunny. Petra had nightmares about the bloody rabbit for weeks. Billy's escapade was the final straw and from then on, he was no longer welcome to join in with our games.

As I sat in my room, I recalled the nightmare I had had over a year prior. I wondered if my nightmare had been a warning of Billy's capabilities. The laughter and blood had an evil resemblance. I shuddered at the thought and picked up my kewpie doll. Holding her tightly between my arms, I skipped out of my room and down the stairs, following the aroma of freshly baked hot cross buns.

My mother was a great cook; there was not as much pre-packaged food in those days, so if you could not cook you often went without. From a young age, I would have to help my mother in the kitchen. Although, for the time education of girls was not viewed as important as education for boys my parents said that they wanted my life to be well balanced. My mother would purchase The Australian Women's Weekly, it was one of the largest weekly papers circulated in Australia and inside it contained interesting news stories, advice columns and recipes. She would select simple recipes, which I would have to cook, then of an evening I would have to sit and read passages from the columns to practice my pronunciation of words and my grammar.

Anzac biscuits, an exciting new biscuit recipe created in early 1920 by a New Zealander had found their way into Australian cook books. These crunchy delights along with chocolate cake were among my favourite recipes. Once in the oven, I would wait patiently, watching the clock and counting down the minutes as they baked. The aroma would fill the house and with the chocolate cake, I was always allowed to lick the mixing bowl as a treat. Ironing was another chore I was given, hankies and tea towels were my first challenge and when I mastered these, I was allowed to do more detailed clothes such as shirts. I only ever burnt one piece of clothing that I can remember, of all things it was one of my father's favourite shirts. For my efforts, I received his leather belt wrapped around my behind.

Although my father was a very casual kind of man, he was a strong believer in discipline and rules. No one could convince him that there were such things as accidents. To him, there was always someone to blame and the strap was received due to my stupidity and carelessness. I was sure at times he enjoyed finding reasons to belt me. It was as if he enjoyed being the one in power.

He was the man of the house and no one was allowed to forget it.

CHAPTER SEVEN

Bugsy's correspondence was always interesting and regular; our friendship grew stronger as each day passed. In Sydney, I continued with my schooling while in Dunberry, Bugsy was doing the same. He also continued to work the land with his father. In my eyes he was no longer a boy, Bugsy was now a fine young man. On my dressing table sat a photo of him. He was a most impressive figure in his Sunday best.

I wrote him a long letter replying to each of his straight away, counting down the days for when we would next see each other. My journey to Dunberry was always looked forward to with great enthusiasm and excitement; I would soon be re-united with Bugsy. Dunberry had become our family holiday spot. A destination we used to escape from Sydney several times a year especially when the annual goat races were running. My parents enjoyed the sereneness Dunberry could offer, while for me, Dunberry represented new and exciting adventures and endless conversations with Bugsy.

Always within a few days of returning, my body, soul and spirit had been revitalised. Each time I returned I would be amazed at the way Paddy was growing. At first, it was her size that was noticeable. In later visits, it was her personality, she was a smart dog. She would assist in the rounding up of the sheep, her commands given to her as a series of whistles. She never forgot me either, even when we were apart for months at a time. Bugsy's father had sold the other pups as they needed the money and could not afford to keep good working dogs just as pets. Other farmers in the area could use the services of a good working dog. They too needed as much help as they could get and a dog was a cheap alternative when it came to running sheep and cattle on the land. After a long day of work Paddy would join us for a swim in the dam, she loved the water, even as a pup she would get excited as we approached the water.

Paddy could sense when things were wrong too. One day, we were swimming in the dam and a black snake slithered through the grass until it found rest in our pile of clothes. If it were not for Paddy I would have been bitten and would have surely died. Leaving the coolness of the dam I walked to the pile of clothes, Paddy stood between me and the clothes barking, as I stretched out my hand she growled. At first, I thought she had turned on me and I feared she might bite. Then I noticed the snake, its body coiled and camouflaged beside Bugsy's boots. By that time Bugsy had gotten out of the dam, he had come to see what the commotion was all about. Taking me by the hand, he pulled me back from harm's way and we ran to fetch his father who rid us of the snake. It was again safe to return to the dam. I rewarded Paddy with a large bone I purchased form the local butcher along with hugs and kisses.

Bugsy was also my hero. His large strong hands had pulled me to safety; words could not express the way I felt. It was as though I had known Bugsy all my life, even longer. I was not sure if I believed in reincarnation or past lives. Nevertheless, I thought, if it was at all true. Then surely, Bugsy and I had met before. Dunberry was merely the site of our reuniting. Sometimes I would sit and think of these things when I was alone; I would plot out in my head the words I would say when I next saw Bugsy. I would tell him how much he meant to me, tell him how I never went a day without him in my thoughts.

He lived so far away, I wondered if I was in his thoughts as much as he was in mine. We were distant friends, everlasting friends, yet to express such feelings could push him away. I assessed all the "what if" scenarios and in the end I was not prepared to lose such a dear friend. The words never left my lips. Trapped by the fear of rejection, I wondered if Bugsy really knew how much he meant to me.

Bugsy was a huge cricket fan and so I begged my parents for the money to buy him a cricket set for his fifteenth birthday. They agreed and I gave it to him when we visited. Calling himself the next Donald Bradman, he would take his bat and ball in front on the water tank and practice hitting for hours at a time. His old cricket bat, which had been carved out of an old log, was thrown on the fire the night he obtained his present. On later visits, he showed me how he had taught Paddy to fetch the ball, this he proclaimed would help in his practicing to hit the ball out of the field. Bugsy never got to play a real competition game of cricket, but it never hurt to dream.

And, dreaming we did, together we would dream of great adventures, to different lands and in different times. We would imagine what it was like to have lived in Australia hundreds of years prior, what it would have been like to have lived as co-inhabitants of a dinosaur planet. To be a great discoverer, like Christopher Columbus or Ferdinand Magellan who had dared to sail where many claimed was the edge of the world. All those years ago so many had accepted the overall belief that the world was flat. Anyone venturing beyond the "edge" would drop into nothingness, literally sail over the edge into a vertical drop. People like these explorers were a testament to human will power. They were brave men, men many considered crazy for they dared to venture beyond beliefs and challenged fears, the worst fear of all, that nothing was out there except disaster. Bugsy and I were young and brave we never wanted to be stuck in our own, "World is flat belief." We wanted to challenge our own beliefs. Our imagination was the gateway to countless experiences; once the gate was opened on an idea both of us would expand and change the experience, as we so desired. The knowledge we gained through reading at school, in subjects like geography and history would come to life, words from our books would jump from the pages. We were able to leap back in time to dates like September 1519 and become two of the two hundred and seventy sailers that set sail with Ferdinand Magellan on his great and exciting voyage around the world. It was a voyage he did not survive after being killed by natives in the Philippine Islands. But, as we closed our eyes we could imagine the challenges that had to be faced, how they would had prayed before embarking on such a voyage. The revolts and mutiny, desertion and dangerous seas. Having to drink water that was slimy and stunk and being forced to eat rats after food ran low. A voyage that would result in only eighteen sailors surviving and four ships being destroyed. When we closed our eyes characters came to life, our surroundings changed and the magical thing was that we could enter or leave wherever, whenever we chose.

As I think back now and recall so many of our imagined adventures, I realise how over the years my ability to dream has decreased. What amazes me is how active a young child's imagination can be yet, as time passes this imagination which was once so vocalised appears to disintegrate with the world around us expecting conversations to consist of facts. In some cases, to the extent where those who verbalise their active imaginations are frowned upon or viewed as weird and disturbed. Then, I must question, are the gifted and lucky individuals those who in their adult years still possess the ability to imagine? When we lose this ability, do we miss countless other experiences? Do our social values ultimately prevent us from tapping into a natural ability we are born with? Should children be encouraged to dream and use their imaginations?

Nancy Drew, Bryce Courtenay, Stephen King, Agatha Christie, Ian Fleming and Sidney Sheldon all great authors with great imaginations. Star Wars, Planet of the Apes, Gone With The Wind, Chitty Chitty Bang Bang, all great movies, none of which are true stories based on facts. The world would be a sad and boring place without these.

I wish I still had the same ability I did as a child. I wish I could tap into my imagination, as I had done so easily so many years ago. These days, my world is so overwhelmed by facts.

CHAPTER EIGHT

1939, Countless numbers of unemployed people roamed Australia in search of work and food. The Great Depression had claimed its victims. The atrocity of war was around us. On the other side of the world Hitler, one of the most brutal dictators in history reigned with terror, his Nazi plague invading Poland. It was the year Australia and New Zealand declared war on Germany, while propaganda flooded our newspapers, claiming the fate of the world was in our hands.

Although, I have never considered my parents wealthy, we were able to maintain a comfortable lifestyle, relatively unscathed by the Depression. I was fifteen and did not fully comprehend the consequences of the actions and events. Late at night, I would lay awake in my bed listening to my parents talking as I had done throughout my life. However, now their voices held expressions of anxiety and worry, expressions they did not convey in my presence.

Each evening after dinner, my parents would retreat to the lounge room and listen to the wireless. My father would read aloud the summary column of The Sydney Morning Herald, while my mother sewed. Air raids, air battles, battle ships sunk, aerial attacks, night attacks, counter-attacks, casualties and killings. These were all subjects raised within their discussions. Occasionally, Mr. Menzies, our Prime Minister addressed the nation. In early December, he urged Australians to, "Face the facts." The real war, he said, had yet to begin.

I couldn't bear to see all the wrong in the world, the heartache, the pain, all the unhappiness. I didn't know what I could do to make things right, what I could do to make people more than just content in their lives. What could I do to end the anxiety and worry from which they could not escape?

Bugsy and I continued to maintain our friendship. His family was hit hard by the depression and his college education was cut short due to lack of money. Many city folk, who had given up on the big smoke, opted to roam the countryside in an effort to find work.Bugsy would write to me telling tales of travellers, with only one swag containing all their worldly possessions. He told me how they had to lock up their chickens, fearing they would end up in the bellies of the hungry nomads. Our friendship so close, yet, our worlds so far apart.

It was in the late December of 1939, just before Christmas that Bugsy came to visit me. It had been just over six months since we last saw each other and it took him two weeks to travel on foot to reach Sydney, working odd jobs along the way to obtain food.He was a welcome sight, my knight in shining armour, my ray of sunshine from behind the clouds that over-shadowed my every move, a young man now eighteen years of age.

Together we sat for days, openly discussing the world as it appeared to us. We had both lost sight of the happier days. It was as if they had been eaten away by the hopelessness of the world, which surrounded us.

I was on school holidays, so in the day we would venture into the city and walk around the harbour. Bugsy was amazed at the Harbour Bridge.

"One day they will let people walk over it." He said.

I laughed his comment seemed absurd. Little did I

know, they actually would. Oh, how I would love to scale the Harbour Bridge. People say it's an amazing feeling and the view you see all over Sydney is spectacular. It's just a shame that my body would not cope with such a huge feat.

That Christmas was a very solemn occasion. Our house, which would normally have been filled with Christmas cheer, stood empty and quiet. Doors bolted and drapes drawn. Paper chains hung around the room; carefully selected decorations along with presents stacked beneath our tree collected dust. There would be no Christmas dinner, no singing of Christmas carols, and no hunting for six-pence in the pudding, which remained hanging in its Muslin bag. My parents were missing.

It happened on a Friday, three days before Christmas. My father never appeared for work that day, never telephoned in to say he was sick, just failed to show. I was the last person known to have seen them, besides several claims of sightings as far away as Dunedoo.

After spending the Friday night alone, I telephoned my aunt Kate at about seven-thirty on Saturday morning to advise her that my parents were gone. At first, she did not understand what I meant. I remember she just kept repeating, "What are you talking about, Shirley? What are you saying?" Finally, I replied with panic, "Please can you come over, I need you!" and I hung up the receiver.

Within minutes, she was at my front door, inside, then on the telephone to the police and to my aunt Margaret who was down visiting from Newcastle and staying at her sister-in-law's house in Waterloo. It was a long day, full of routine questions. When did I last see them? What were they wearing? Had there been an argument? Countless questions, that went on and on. As far as anyone could work out, my parents woke Friday morning, showered, dressed, ate breakfast and went for an early morning stroll, from which they never returned.

When the detectives finished their questioning, I was extremely rattled; I had never spoken to a police officer before and had always associated a visit from the law with a person being thrown into jail. Police officers had paid Billy a visit earlier that year during class and he had been taken away. Rumours went round the neighbourhood that Billy had been thrown in jail. I did not want to go to jail. Both detectives were very pleasant and understanding, they wanted to help me find my parents. But the sight of their uniforms, the guns and handcuffs gave me the creeps. All through my life, I experienced the same feeling whenever I came face to face with an officer of the law. Maybe this ongoing feeling was a result of my childhood experience, I guess everyone suffers a similar feeling when approached by an officer of the law. Why, even seeing a police car while innocently driving along can result in a quick glance of the speedometer and a feeling of guilt that we have just been caught exceeding the speed limit.

After my questioning was complete, the detectives interviewed my neighbour Mrs. Knightly who had been called upon to come over. She was an elderly lady, probably close to seventy-five at the time. Unfortunately, for the detectives Mrs. Knightly was not of any assistance. She was almost completely deaf and half-blind. Mrs. Knightly spent many hours outside pottering around in her garden, especially in the cool hours of the morning. She told the officers that she may have seen my parents but could not be sure if it was on the Friday morning or maybe it was at another time. Any clues would have been of assistance in solving the mystery. However, Mrs. Knightly's vagueness could never result in what could have been referred to as substantial or reliable evidence.

Mr. Cummings, my other neighbour was away on holidays at the time of my parent's disappearance and so the detectives advised that they would commence a door knock to other houses in my neighbourhood.

As they left my house to start the door knocking I took myself outside and sat on the front verandah watching their every move. It was getting close to lunchtime and the summer sun had a real bite in it so after a few minutes I retreated inside and headed to the kitchen in search for something to quench my thirst. My throat was very dry and without a cold drink, I feared I would collapse.

Walking down the hallway, towards the kitchen I noticed the door to the lounge had been pulled closed. Intrigued by this action and with the sound of muffled voices I paused for a moment, listening to see if I could identify whom they belonged to. It was my two aunts and a welfare officer who had arrived with the police. It appeared; they were discussing my living arrangements. The welfare officer was stating that irrespective as to the situation of my missing parents it was not appropriate under any circumstances for a young girl of fifteen years to be left alone. All three were very concerned about my welfare and my state of mind. I heard Aunt Kate talking, she insisted she would be more than capable of looking after me, stating that moving in with her would mean I would be close to home when or if my parents returned. Aunt Margaret appeared to agree, she did not want to give me any additional pressure and a move out of the area could result in unnecessary stress. Relocation to Newcastle would be far too much of an upheaval.

Crouching next to the door, my eavesdropping became more intent as the welfare office talked about her responsibility, which included looking at all options. Whilst she acknowledged the presence of two aunties. She had to investigate the possibility of other relatives, who may also be a viable option. That was when I heard Aunt Kate's voice raise.

"Oh shit!" she exclaimed.

This was followed by what seemed a long pause.

"Mum, I haven't told Mum! Bloody hell! This is going to give her another thing to whinge about!"

The next voice I heard was that of aunt Margaret, reassuring her everything would be fine and that she was sure grandma Edna would understand given the circumstances.

"Come on Kate, don't worry. I will let Mum know what is happening."

"But, what will you say?"

"Look, it will be okay, I will let her know." Aunt Margaret continued with her reassuring.

Grandma Edna! I thought, *what will Grandma Edna think? What will I do if the decision is made that I should live with her?*Surely, the idea was inconceivable. Overcome by a wave of nausea, I was forced to place my hands on the floor to prevent myself from falling over. Surely, they would not send me to live with Grandma Edna. She was old, grouchy, stubborn, extremely cantankerous and at times unpredictable not to mention closed off to the world. I was young, I needed fresh air, surely they would not think I deserved to be sent away. Not with Grandma Edna, not with Fummy her stinking old ratty cat that hissed and growled when I came near.

Grandma Edna would not want me. I would be

imposing on her life, and to her I would be nothing more than a burden. Reassuring myself of these facts, I again focused my attention towards their discussion.

By this stage, the conversation had progressed back to the proposal of living with Aunt Kate. It appeared Grandma Edna and Aunt Margaret had been ruled out on the basis they both lived too far away. And so, behind closed doors with no input from me it was decided I would live with Aunt Kate as she also lived in Paddington.

The detectives finished their door knock later that afternoon and although their investigation had been reasonably extensive, all their efforts had proved fruitless. It was also in the afternoon that Bugsy returned to my house. He too was questioned; however, he was unable to offer any information to assist in their inquiries. He was merely visiting from Dunberry and although he had seen my parents since his arrival in Sydney a week ago, for the last few days he had been at Parramatta working and looking at farming equipment.

Detective Stone, engaged in a lengthy conversation with Bugsy, as it turned out he too had relatives from Dunberry. Unable to assist with inquiries and wanting to please Bugsy promised he would pass on the detectives best regards for the festive season to his relatives. After they completed their discussions Bugsy came to my side, he embraced me and promised that he would keep me in his thoughts then he departed, this time for the long walk back to Dunberry.

Overwhelmed by the situation, my aunts still engrossed within private conversations and with Bugsy vanishing from sight as he turned the corner I retreated to my bedroom. The world was spinning. Although the earth as we all know it turns and rotates around the sun, its forces only seen not felt, at this very moment it was as if I could feel every fraction of this great centrifugal force. It is a fact that the earth rotates at about one thousand miles an hour, this rotational force seemed to be magnified at an uncontrollable rate, external pressures consumed my body. My parents were missing, they were really gone and my world was collapsing. Lying on my bed I broke down and cried as I had never cried before. What was happening? War, destruction, death, loss, all of a sudden my head began pounding, knots twisted and turned within my stomach. The only way I could describe my feeling would be as to say I felt as though my stomach contained hundreds of snakes twisting and turning within themselves, trying to escape from my emotionally tortured body.

Perspiration dripped from my forehead, as I barely made it to the bathroom. I clung to the toilet bowl spewing out what felt like the entire contents of my innards. I was in shock. The vomiting was like a pressure gauge being released, once complete.Although, for a short while I felt a slight relief, I had to come to grips with myself. The facts of the whole ordeal would not vanish. I was not temporarily trapped within a bad dream, my nightmare was real - my parents were gone, that is what was happening.

As I sit here and type away, it appears to me that no matter who disappears from where, there are nearly always claims of sightings. No sightings of my parents were ever substantiated and police thought many may have been given by pranksters or those who honestly believed distant figures could belong to the parents of a distraught fifteen-year-old.

Once all urges to vomit subsided, I returned to my

bedroom and collapsed on my bed. The focus of my thoughts clearly fixed on my parents. My mother had always been loving and caring; she was generally quiet and submissive to my father, never game enough to go against his word or voice objections to his opinions. Over recent times, I had watched her generally optimistic ways vanish, overrun by worry and her fear of a happy future lost forever. My father, also experienced attitudinal changes over recent times. Although, I was not close to my father, as he always seemed to hold himself remote, I could feel the atmosphere, which surrounded us all changing. This was not a good feeling. I had explained these feelings and changes within my parents to the detectives. Taking notes they were interested in all details, I could offer.

After some time, Aunt Kate came to my room. In a soft and consoling voice, she explained that she would gather some clothes and together we would go to her house. It had been arranged and agreed I would stay with her. Aunt Kate spoke as she packed clothes in a bag; her words going in one ear and out the other, as my thoughts remained fixed on my parents. When her packing was complete, she ushered me downstairs and into her car for the short drive.

Arriving at her house, she led me upstairs and instructed me that I should lay down and rest while she prepared me a snack. Although I told her I could not eat anything, she insisted that she would make me a sandwich and bring a drink. Something in my belly would do me well. When she left the room, I stood at the base of the bed my back towards it, taking a deep sigh I fell backwards and sunk into the soft mattress. The linen contained a musty smell; it was obviously a guest's room, which had not been used for some time. Sitting up, I removed my shoes, threw them to the corner of the room and flopped backwards. Repeatedly, I said to myself that I had to relax and breath. Repeatedly, I told myself that I was safe and everything would be fine. Aunt Kate returned within minutes, placing a sandwich and glass of milk on the bedside table. She told me that she would leave so I could rest, while she completed some business. Leaving the room she turned back towards me and assured me that things would be fine and told me that should I need anything then I should not hesitate to call her. I nodded, acknowledging her kindness with a half smile.

Alone again, my thoughts continued to wander. I did not even attempt to eat the food Aunt Kate prepared. My stomach would not settle and I did not dare touch anything, no matter how appealing and well presented it appeared. Aunt Kate came into check on me; it was getting late as the sun was going down. Sitting on the side of the bed she stroked my forehead and again assured me that things would be fine. Tears welled in my eyes, squeezing them tightly I felt the warmth of my tears run down the side of my face and onto my pillow. Again, my uncontrollable crying commenced. Rolling onto my side and away from my aunt I grasped the pillow from above my head pulling it down in front of my body as I assumed the foetal position. Aunt Kate rubbed my side, I could tell she was lost for words and so she said her good nights. On the bedside table, there was a clock and lamp. Rising from the bed, she switched on the lamp. That first night, the light remained on while my thoughts whizzed from one thing to another; the day just passed, the previous day, the last conversations with my parents, last Christmas. I was trying to rationalise my feelings, trying to place points of time and events into perspective. The clock was driving me crazy, tick-tock, tick-tock. Reaching over from the bed I grabbed the clock, jumped from the bed, opened the window and threw it out. I needed to think. The bloody clock was driving me crazy.

CHAPTER NINE

The next morning, I awoke and ventured down to the kitchen where I found Aunt Kate talking with Aunt Margaret. Aunt Margaret was expressing some concern for their mother's state of mind. Apparently, when she broke the news of my parent's disappearance, Grandma Edna launched into an erratic attack as to who was to blame. Initially, she announced that both had been recruited for war efforts. Then, she swiftly changed this explanation claiming it was the Germans who were responsible. Calling those responsible for their disappearance, Nazi bastards and Jew haters. Aunt Margaret had no idea where the Jew haters came into the equation but told Aunt Kate that she had acknowledged the news and within minutes had reverted back to her normal complaining. Her delusional rants and irrational thinking made me thankful that I had not been sent to her.

Soon after my arriving at Aunt Kate's, I was introduced to Stella, a young woman in her early twenties. Initially, our introductions were done over the telephone. The first quality I recognised was the articulate manner in which she spoke, reflecting a kind, thoughtful and understanding personality. In person, her smile and caring eyes radiated a powerful allure. I was not sure what part she played within my aunts life but I could tell by their actions they were very close and of kindred spirit. Stella was an adorable gal. Like Aunt Kate, I felt an instant liking to her. She was a bright, talented and intelligent woman who possessed irrepressible optimism and a vivacious personality. She was always ready for a joke and good laugh and Stella loved the social scene. Humorous, authentic, respectful and trustworthy, at times reserved but eternally gracious, an attractive and beautiful woman. Stella was much shorter than Aunt Kate, more of a stocky build but not fat. Her laughter was infectious and she had nicknames for many. Referring to Aunt Kate as, "Miss Indy" short for Miss Independence, it was a name she said should make Aunt Kate feel proud. Her theory was that being independent in life was a great achievement. Far too many women she believed lived on the backs of their husbands, far too many could not stand on their own two feet even in an emergency. Enjoying the company of others was one thing, but to need them for survival was down right ridiculous.

Bugsy made it back to Dunberry just in time for the New Year. By that time, I had my own room sorted at Aunt Kate's. Adapting to her way of life was more difficult than I had first anticipated. Her demeanour and attitude towards the world and those in it made her appear worlds apart from my parents. I needed Aunt Kate; I needed to be with someone of such independence and individualism. She was open-minded and understanding. She accepted others for who they were and was not afraid of showing her unconditional love. My world had been turned upside down with my parent's departure; I had made a transition into what appeared a New World - one full of feelings and attitudes I had rarely felt.

I embraced Aunt Kate; I embraced the world around me, yet I never allowed myself to get too close. Always at a safe distance from everyone, expect Bugsy. He was the only person who I allowed to get a little closer.

He understood me; he understood what I was going through. Although, he had never experienced the loss of his parents, he had experienced loss within his life. Being around the same age, I felt comfort in his words.

Bugsy wrote to me early in the New Year. He was concerned about me. At the beginning of the letter, he wrote that I had never left his thoughts since he departed, how we had stood united and how he would never let me down in my time of need. I recalled the hug he had given me when he was leaving, his strong arms around body, his chest against mine; he made me feel safe.

I replied straight away and told him that he too had been in my thoughts and I thanked him for his support in my time of need.

Bugsy also wrote that on his arrival back home he found his father stuck in bed. He had suffered a farming accident, the tractor had tipped and he had been pinned below it for over an hour before he was discovered. Normally Bugsy would have been there however, when the accident occurred he was with me in Sydney. He would not be able to return to Sydney for some time. This saddened me, but I understood that he had certain obligations, which he had to keep. His father was lucky to come out of the accident with only a broken leg; many farmers died in such accidents, come to think of it many farmers still die from farming accidents.

Bugsy loved the farm, when he visited me in Sydney he would always say there is a difference in the air. Country air is so clean and sweet smelling, in the city the air is dense, full of pollution. On the other hand, I was a city girl. I enjoyed my holidays in the country, but as for farming, I would tell Bugsy my hand is not going to end up the back of any cow, no matter how much strife it is in. He would laugh and tell me that one of these days he would show me what real work was all about, not like the chores I said I had to do.

Before I knew it, the new school year commenced. At first, I felt strange going to school from Aunt Kate's house. I did not realise my parent's disappearance would impact as greatly as it did. Many of my school friends appeared to distance themselves from me. I presumed they did not know what to talk about, as they all knew that my parents were missing. For the first few weeks of the school term, I would spend my lunchtime alone. My after school routine also changed when I went to stay with Aunt Kate. I rarely ventured outside to meet friends, choosing to read instead. Once I completed my homework, I would stroll out to the backyard and sit by the pond; here I would let my thoughts drift away to another place, another time, a happier time. I missed my parents more than I had ever thought I would, seldom did I speak, someone else always started conversations.

Sometimes, Aunt Kate would come and join me by the pond. She was concerned about the absence of company and would constantly ask me how I was, what was I thinking, did I need to talk to anyone or could she help me at all. On many occasions, I felt I should talk, I should say what I was thinking, but then something inside of me would prevent me from doing so. I did not say what I was thinking as I feared I would be rejected by the one person who meant the world to me. At home with my parents, I was rarely asked for an opinion or to share a thought. On the rare occasion that I had, my father would pounce on me, instructing me to grow up or to be sensible.

The pond possessed a special splendour, which had

only ever been equalled to that found in Dunberry. It was large and beautiful, on sunny days I would have to squint as I approached its edge, the suns rays reflecting off the tranquil water.

As I sat, I would watch butterflies elegantly hover around the surrounding flowerbeds, joined by the occasional dragonflies with their wings flapping furiously. Birds chirping and singing were the only noises that could be heard at the water edge and so I would lie there my body cushioned by the soft green grass below. Thoughts drifting away, my body relaxed.

By the time the second school term arrived, some of my old school friends had regained their confidence in being able to approach me and conduct conversations. However, these conversations lacked the depth they had had before my parent's disappearance. Outings with their parents became outings. Treats or cakes their mothers cooked became treats or cakes. It was as if they thought by not mentioning their parents, I would not think of mine. They tried to do what they thought was right, but, they did not understand; no one understood the way I felt.

As time went by, I found comfort in solitude, that way no one would have to concern him or herself with watching their words. For a brief moment, I wondered if it might have been better had I gone to stay with Aunt Margaret, that way no one would have known about my parents. New friendships would have developed and no one would have been afraid of me. No one would have felt they needed to tiptoe around me, in fear they may upset me by rekindling thoughts of my missing parents. However, that was a short-lived thought. Ultimately living with Aunt Margaret would have sent me batty. She had tendencies to talk to me in stupid baby voices and I was sure living with her would have sent me around the twist.

Without any prior notice, Bugsy turned up at Aunt Kate's in late June; it had been just over six months since we last saw each other. On his last visit, the circumstances had been very difficult. It was a pleasant surprise to see his face when I opened the front door. Although Aunt Kate never admitted that she had organised his visit, I was sure she had full knowledge of his plan prior to the doorbell ringing. Normally, she answered the front door, however on this occasion she instructed me to do so. Wrapping my arms around my welcome surprise, I motioned him to come in. Aunt Kate was in her study painting and when I showed her Bugsy all she said was, "Oh my, what a pleasant surprise." She was far too casual acting not to have known something. Placing her brush down she told me to take Bugsy to the other guest room where he could place his bags while she fixed us all a drink and some afternoon tea.

Bugsy stayed with us for one week, not a lot was discussed about my parents. Most of the time, he just expressed his concerns about my state of mind. Within our recent correspondence, he said that he had noticed a distance and he wanted to assure me that he would always be there for me in my times of need. This was something that I knew, as he had proved this on several occasions. I was saddened at the thought of this distance and assured him that I had been unaware of the changes he spoke of. It was obviously occurring on a subconscious level.

The world was a dark and dismal place. I hated life as it was, not that I wanted to end my life I just wished that there was some way to bring back the happier times. The war was still around us. I wanted desperately to escape, but knew there was no way out. There was no way to go back. No way to change the current situation. No matter how hard I closed my eyes and tried to imagine, it was not possible. My parents were gone, and the world was constantly changing. I was like a little boat in a big ocean; my ocean was suffering the effects of a very bad storm. I had to hang in there and ride the waves.

During the day, we would venture into Sydney and stroll around the shops or on the warmer days we would just lay by the pond in the sun and talk the hours away. Aunt Kate was happy to have Bugsy stay, she was happy to see me communicating without appearing to be under duress. Her intentions were good and I was glad she was happy.

When it was time for Bugsy to leave I cried. He was my confidante, my strength and my world. Without him, I was lost and I soon slipped back into depression.

CHAPTER TEN

By the time, it was 1941, my depression had grown and Aunt Kate feared I was not acting as rashly as a seventeen-year-old should. Advising me that she was acting in my best interests, she employed the services of a psychiatrist. Times were still hard for so many, yet Aunt Kate was far from being short of money. Wanting to keep her happy, I attended sessions weekly. I would lie on his lounge, sharing with him only those details I expected Aunt Kate would like to hear. I was sure he would pass on any information, no matter how much he assured me of his doctor / patient confidentially.

Most of the time, I would discuss Bugsy; I would reminisce over the happy days with my parents and our trips to Dunberry. I was living in my own self-induced isolation and even Dr. Black with all his qualifications was not going to break down the barriers I had built around me. In the event, however, that he would ask me a direct question to which I did not want to reply I would go off on a tangent talking about the weather, the war or anything else which sprang to mind.

Dr. Black, was an older man in his fifties and his eldest son had gone off to war. At that time, he was posted somewhere in North Africa. I would use this knowledge to assist in my digression from subjects I did not want to talk about. Dr. Black had already lost his younger brother to war and it wouldn't take long for him to lose his train of thought when I mentioned his son. It wasn't that he was no good at his job. It was more so that I knew exactly how to manipulate the situation.

To people, the war had brought grief and sorrow. Although, there was also a sense of pride knowing that fathers, sons and brothers were risking or had given their lives for something greater than themselves. They were defending or had defended what was right. I could see the pain on Dr. Black's face; I could see the worry in his eyes. Although I did not disclose much information within my sessions, I always left feeling better than I had when I entered.

Aunt Kate was pleased that I showed no resistance in going to the sessions. After the first few, I began to look forward to them. To me they became something of a game. As I lay on the lounge, I would study Dr. Black's face. I was amazed how his expressions would change so rapidly when I mentioned the war. I wondered if he studied my face, in the same way when he asked questions.

Between sessions, I would sit in my room and look in the mirror studying my face. I would stare expressionless into the mirror for hours at a time. I became so obsessed with my expressions and the hiding of my feelings that I would look into any mirror that I passed. Even when we went shopping, I would look at my reflection in windows just to make sure I remained expressionless. With all the pain in the world around me and all the other people with their problems, I did not want to be another problem on the pile.

Aunt Kate being the person she was hosted many parties. The lounge would be full of socialites and people from all walks of life. All laughing, talking and drinking. Some of their jokes were funny and the room would erupt into laughter, I would stand straight-faced, expressionless.

Sometimes I would laugh; however, it was not at their jokes. I was laughing at the facades most hid behind. Take for instance, Norma Jones. She would enter a room larger than life with her head held high in the air, all the airs and graces until of course she consumed large amounts of alcohol. After more than just a couple of drinks, the real action started and the true Norma was revealed. She would whip off her precious silver fox fur coat, throw her shoes off and burst into song. Norma knew how to party and could drink with the best of them. She would proudly boast about her connections to those within the sly grog trade and to individuals who could assist her in acquiring those hard to find items. She was only to happy to organise delivery of what she referred to as *precious cargo or liquid gold.*

I remember one night after having a few too many, good old Norma ended up in the pond, clothes and all. When she emerged, from under the water, her white dress clung to her body and beneath she was wearing nothing. All she could say was, "Oh no, Normies you seem to have found the pond." This I did find amusing. Especially, when Aunt Kate and Stella tried to rescue Norma and they too ended up in the pond. They were all screaming and splashing about in the water and with it coming into winter, I imagined it would have felt quite icy.

As I stood there staring, my laughter had vanished and again my face became expressionless. Aunt Kate screamed at me to go and get some towels. Hearing her screams, I casually turned and without saying a word, went to the linen cupboard. By the time I made it back to the pond, a crowd had gathered to offer assistance and the three had climbed out looking like drowned rats.

All of Norma's elegance had been washed from her. The antics she displayed after a few too many drinks were definitely not the behaviour becoming of a lady. Before me stood a woman who was revealing more than just her entire body, she was also now just as plain as an average person you would pass on the street. Maybe a little wetter than most.

I enjoyed Aunt Kate's parties, mostly for the variety of guests. In my mind, I would make up little stories, which would go along with their behaviour. I would imagine what they did for a living. On many occasions, my guesses would be correct. I could always distinguish the want-to-be actors for they were always the ones paying the loudest compliments to the movie directors and or known actors. On the other hand, many painters and artists could be seen gathered together discussing works of art or being overly friendly to art critics and museum owners.

Many guests, were just wealthy socialites. Norma was a woman who had married into great wealth; she had risen above the streets from where she once lived. From what I understood, she had met her husband when she was only about seventeen and he was in his late fifties. He revelled in the fact that he had a beautiful young girl on his arms and showered her with gifts. Now coming from the streets and not wanting to return there Norma did everything in her power to please the old man and within months they were married. Soon after that, he was dead. Good old Norma inherited the lot. Of course, there were many rumours about the real cause of his death but ultimately his death certificate said acute myocardial infarction or heart attack. And that was how Norma got her money.

She was the exception to the rule; most of the wealthy guests actually worked hard for their money and did possess a certain class even after they consumed large amounts of alcohol. Nevertheless, she did offer amusement, as they all did in their different ways.

The parties were always very entertaining and educational. During many of them, I would grab a glass of wine in one hand and just drift from one conversation to another, listening to anything that sounded interesting. Aunt Kate was happy to let me have the occasional glass of wine. She said it was an education for me. Better to have me try alcohol while in the safety of our house, rather than out in some sleazy pub or party when I reached the legal drinking age.

CHAPTER ELEVEN

1942, A feeling of coldness engulfed my body. I was alone and I did not trust anyone. I could not confide in anyone. Bugsy was gone. Bugsy my eternal friend, the first boy I had ever kissed was gone forever. Aunt Kate embraced me as we sat on the sofa. Her soft hands caressing my hair, my face buried in her bosom. I was speechless; my words had been stolen just as Bugsy had been stolen. The police had just paid us a visit, to deliver the news of yet another loss I would experience within my life. I was only nearing eighteen years of age. Yet, already I was without parents and now I had lost my closest friend. My knight in shining armour, the man whom had been able to send me those rays of sunshine from behind the clouds that over-shadowed my every move. He was only twenty-one.

The police officer was very sympathetic to my feelings. Detective Stone had remembered me from my parents disappearance three years before. He had remembered the closeness Bugsy and I had shared.

Detective Stone, said Bugsy's car had careered of the road and down an embankment. His death would have been instantaneous; it appeared he might have lost control. I sat there still embraced within my aunt Kate's arms. Bugsy was not the type of man who would lose control at the wheel - I knew there had to be much more behind his death.

He had been in Sydney, only weeks before his death. He had come to the big smoke for a long deserved break.

The effects of the Depression still surrounded us, yet with him by my side nothing else really mattered. I had not realised exactly how much I had meant to Bugsy until he proposed to me. I was shocked. Yes, I did love him. He had done so much for me. However, I could not love a man the way in which I thought I should, without first being able to love myself. I had very low self-esteem and I did not accept his proposal.I know he was upset, I know my response had hurt him maybe more than he had ever been hurt, so I sat there with him in silence. Oh, the silence, it was almost deafening.

Silence, very much like that I experienced while sitting there on the sofa with Aunt Kate. I freed myself from Aunt Kate's arms and retreated to my bedroom. Aunt Kate was caring, she was open-minded, understanding and she accepted others for who they were, loving unconditionally, which made her seem worlds apart from my parents, yet I could not confide in her as I had with Bugsy. I lay on my bed for hours, crying and thinking only of Bugsy, trying to imagine what may have been running through his mind, in the final moments of his life. I wondered if he thought about all those what if scenarios, which frequently infiltrated our minds. I wondered, if only for a split second he changed his mind, however, he had already passed the point of no return. I am sure you would think of your family, friends, life experiences and incomplete dreams, if you knew they would soon be gone - I wondered what he was thinking, I still do wonder what he was thinking.

Had his mind wandered back to the first time we met, to our virginal kiss, to the laughter and fun times we shared? Trampling through the bush together, at many times we had said that it was as if we were the only inhabitants. Had Bugsy recalled these moments? What about how not long after we first met, we had found a tired old piece of rope and transformed the local water hole into a splashing pool filled with hype and activity. Children flocked from miles around, year in and year out for a turn to leap from the banks. The rope suspended from an overhanging branch, grasped firmly between their hands as they flew out releasing their hands and screaming, their bodies splashing into the water with cheers and laughter.

Then there were the many times we held hands, as we walked along the riverbank. Our nights of painful sunburn, suffered from hours and hours of adventures, of swimming and fishing along the river. Bugsy always held the record for catching the most fish; he also held the record for catching socks. I recalled the day we went fishing and he caught not one but two socks, within a matter of minutes. When he pulled out the second, I laughed so hard I feared I may wet myself and once our laughter subsided, he swore me to secrecy in fear of embarrassment. That was one thing we could do, keep secrets and that was a great part of what formed our wonderful relationship. To tell another secrets and trust in their word was an amazing thing, something to be cherished. I never told anyone about the socks, a secret was a secret and together we had many.

But, then again, everyone interprets situations in different ways. I recalled the warmth and caring I felt in Bugsy's presence. Had I also conveyed the same feeling? I hoped Bugsy's feelings were a reflection of my own. I hoped that the time we shared for him had brought equal happiness and joy. Our laughter, his laughter, our smiles, his smile. Surely, they were images in my mind created through true and memorable events. I found myself questioning the realism of my thoughts. To understand and accept that someone may propose marriage does not necessarily mean that they too share an equalled love. I did love Bugsy and yes he had wanted to marry me. However, for what reason? Was I just a safe bet, to him? Was I just an individual in which he found comfort, everyone likes comfort? Or, was I more?

Looking up, I found myself examining the ceiling. The only answers it offered were brush strokes and patches within the plasterwork, reminisce of repairs and facelifts the house had endured over time. People are like houses, they all possess individual characteristics, they all need the occasional bandaid and make over, and they all crave attention and care. Had I expressed enough of all these things to Bugsy, or had my actions resulted in the consequences of his? No one likes rejection, some things in life can consume the mind and cloud judgements. Some things, which start out with good intentions, can inadvertently result in disastrous endings. I hoped that my interaction with Bugsy had not altered what was his originally intended fate, for every action within our life there is a reaction. We had met like lines on a road map, together we travelled, sporadically we experienced separation yet we always reunited, we had experienced all the highs and lows like hills and gullies. Now Bugsy had fallen and I too had taken a tumble as I found myself in a deep sea of sadness.

"No!" I yelled, "No!" My voice echoed around the room. I wanted to turn back, if only I could turn back time and we could change the path on which we had subconsciously chosen to travel. But, what would I choose to change, even if I had the chance? Would everything be better, if we had not met at all or would I have still met another Bugsy, maybe in the form of Richard or Thomas, who would have filled the same shoes? Fate, it was all fate, I was living life as it was intended, maybe it had already been decided upon the birth of Bugsy, that he would depart at such a young age. I had to be happy, I had to appreciate the moments, accept events as they were and continue on with life. We must experience bad times so we can appreciate good. Bugsy had been responsible for a huge portion of good and that was something I had to be thankful and grateful for.

I lay sobbing in my room, until I decided I should take pen to paper and write a poem for Bugsy, a poem I would read at his funeral;

Good-bye

The pain is all over, the suffering has gone,
And to all of the memories we must hold on,
A loved one has departed and we will miss them so much,
Their smile, their voice, all their love and their tender touch.

Though the person has gone, the memories will stay,
And little things will remind us of them both at night and at day,
The pain and sadness of them leaving has touched you and me,
And as their spirit surrounds us, they are floating and free.

In a moment of silence we look to the sky,

Thinking of the good times, we say our good-bye,
At the moment we grieve as we know it's the end,
We will miss them so much, our relative, our friend.

People will live, then people will die,
There always comes a day when we all say
Good-bye.

Bugsy's parents were devastated. Gone with him, were so many of their hopes and dreams. Dreams of the future, which they had held onto ever since his birth. There would be no son to continue on the farming way. No grandchild, no happy ever after.

I never told a soul about Bugsy's proposal and after leaving Dunberry the day after his funeral I never talked about him in any detail until now. I never returned to Dunberry and never found out what became Mr. and Mrs. Smith or Paddy, the dog Bugsy had named especially for me.

My life back in Paddington returned to it's mundane ways, the ongoing war over shadowed everyday life. Air shelters were popping up everywhere, as families were encouraged to build their own at home. Aunt Kate recruited volunteers from around the neighbourhood to lend a helping hand and construct our very own Anderson Shelter in the back yard. Made from galvanised corrugated steel, it arrived in prefabricated kit form. Six curved panels bolted together formed the top with three panels either side that helped formed the main body of the shelter. Final construction saw the securing of two more straight panels fixed to each end, one of which contained a door protected by a wall of earth and steps leading down into the shelter. While each panel was not too heavy for one man to lift, the process of construction entailed several people all working together as the panels were awkward to fix. Buried half in the ground with earth heaped on top, it was well camouflaged and provided almost complete safety except from a direct hit. The Anderson Shelter was designed to accommodate up to six people. It was six feet or just under two metres high, four feet six inches or just under one and a half metres wide and just over six feet or two metres long. Internal fitting out was left up to the owners. Ours contained bunk beds and a storage area for food, water, some board games and a deck of cards and some books. Aunt Kate insisted that while we should always hope for the best, it was only sensible to prepare for the worst. Safety was paramount; thus, her decision to purchase the Anderson Shelter in contrast to other trench shelters, which used concrete for the sides and roof, as these were inherently unstable when, exposed to the effects of an explosion.

Those in Sydney lived in real fear of air raids, not just in the day but at night too. The Japanese would occasionally shell major cities like Sydney from submarines. The level of anxiety was evident along the coastline. Some chose to leave and move to the country in order to stay safe. Sydney ran on low lights at night. If the sirens sounded and wardens could see lights within your house, they would bang on the door demanding you sealed your curtains properly and turn your lights down.

I recall being woken by Aunt Kate's panicked bellowing on more than a few occasions. Hearing the air raid sirens echo or the rattling of gunfire, as I struggled to get dressed before heading to the back yard. They were very frightening times. On one particular occasion,

I am not sure if it was when the Jap subs entered Sydney Harbour but I think it was. I was in a dead sleep, when at first, I was disturbed by these various alarms and the siren sounding. When the alarms sounded, everyone was supposed to go to their shelters, jump under their bed or hide under the kitchen table or whatever. I remember seeing the lights. The lights going across night sky. The searchlights. I can see that in my memory. The searchlight lights going across the night sky. Aunt Kate always kept a tiny little oil lamp in my bedroom; I don't know how it would sit. It was sort of fixed up near the ceiling. On this night, Aunt Kate had been to the pictures when an announcement came over that Sydney was being attacked. The pictures were closed down and everyone went racing home. I remember the door opening, by that time I was upright and had gathered my shoes and I was about to gather my over coat that always hung on the back of the door for easy access. Aunt Kate insisted it always be hung there, in case of such events. Well Aunt Kate came in; she was terribly flustered. For some reason, poor Aunt Kate in her terrified state dashed straight passed my overcoat and went to my drawers rummaging around in the dimness demanding that I tell her where I had left my overcoat. I can still see her. Poor Aunt Kate was just terrified, you see she had been exposed to so many more things in life. She knew individuals who had experienced the First World War in London. She had heard the awful stories from London, with the bombs dropping and she was absolutely terrified of it. Her fear was intensified, by the stories she had heard and she was having a huge panic attack of what could happen but nothing was happening, that was the funny part about it, absolutely nothing happened to us. It was purely the thought of what could happen; there she was struggling like crazy, searching for my coat that was not even in my drawers, rummaging around like mad woman to get me down to the air raid shelter.

Well, eventually we did get there, coat and all. I was terrified of the air raid shelter because there were spiders; the spiders from the garden loved the air raid shelter. That night it was such a performance, I don't believe I will ever forget it. You could hear other voices from the neighbourhood, from people directing operations, telling people where they should go and what they should do. After the sirens, the all clear went or people got fed up with it. I can still remember Aunt Kate saying, "I am going up to make a cup of tea."

But, as I say whether that was the night of the Japanese subs, I am not completely certain, I am assuming it was.

I suppose we were lucky really to have our own shelter. Aunt Kate was very good in that way. I don't think many other people had gone to that much trouble. It was hard work digging a shelter out of ground that consisted of a lot of sand and rock. Although, she had enlisted assistance she too got in to get the job done. She always ensured we only had the best and had our shelter properly lined, it was amazing.

Nearby, the local Council or whoever had dug out shelters at various points through the local park. Many people used to go into those shelters, some didn't bother. The trouble with those shelters, was that all the local alcoholics would congregate in there and of course pee all over the place, so they reeked, they were shocking. People would pack in like sardines, some people took supplies. The shelters were dark; cold at times damp places. Those who were religious would sit in darkness gabbling away saying prayers. Mothers with babies would struggle to keep them silent. Everyone was waiting for silence to descend, for the all clear to be given. The shelters definitely offered a far greater sense of security as opposed to staying inside your house.

In Sydney, the landscape really transformed with the looming fear of air attacks from the Japanese. Signs were erected in Sydney to show the way to your nearest tunnel or shelter that had been set up. Loud speakers were mounted on buildings to broadcast air raid warning sirens. Even the old Sydney General Post Office, on the corner of Pitt Street and Martin Place had air raid protection erected around it. Timber slats covered its once thick stonework and wide sloping awnings were made to protect pedestrians as they entered. Construction on the new St. James Railway station in Sydney also halted. Inside the tunnels originally planned for the Eastern Suburbs line were modified to serve as a public Air Raid shelter. It was a time to take the threats seriously; the removal of street signs was completed in preparation of invasion. Barbed wire defences were also strung across many East Coast beaches to assist in the prevention of attack. Blackout restrictions were enforced, windows were covered with brown paper and netting. Children at school performed air raid drills each morning and were issued with identity tags in case they had to be evacuated to a safer place. Schoolyards had deep trenches with concrete walls. Children would be ushered into the trenches, where they would sit on seats that ran along the walls as wardens wearing gas masks and metal helmets supervised. Air raid precaution instructions, along with accompanying photographs were forwarded to daily and weekly newspapers for publications so that all

Australians would be prepared for Japanese air attacks. Even buses were camouflaged with brown, green and black paint. Aunt Kate, while being ever reassuring insisted that I keep my travels to a minimum.

The government had previously introduced petrol rationing not long, after the War commenced. Now every civilian had to register to get an identity card then produce the identity card to be issued with a ration book from the rationing book issuing centre, which contained a number of coupons. Ration books, were designed for adults, children aged five to nine years old and children under five years. Instructions were very clear. Each ration book contained one hundred and twelve coupons, at the end of the year used coupon booklets were exchanged for new ones. It was imperative to plan spending, as once the coupon was spent it was a yearlong wait for the next to be issued.In 1942, the items on ration were increased, in April 1942 all Australians over the age of nine were required to register with a corner store that was their tea supplier. This allowed those registered to purchase a mere half a pound or about two hundred grams of tea that was expected to last five weeks. This was because of the Japanese capturing and occupying Malaya, the Dutch East Indies and Java, all prime tea producers for Australia. Australians were encourage to sacrifice and go without, smoke less – burn less money, drink less – satisfy a need not habit, give up cosmetics – its smart to be natural. The message was, "save and save Australia."

In May 1942, the government announced it would impose rationing on clothes in coming months. Mass hysteria gripped the women of Australia, stampede buying depleted stocks making blankets and other articles virtually unobtainable. When this rationing was imposed, clothing shops were restricted to only seventy five percent of daily sales, once this quota was reached sales had to be stopped.

The fear of scarcity resulted in hysteria; rumours spread about items individuals feared would be next on the ration list. At one stage, there was a rumour about matches of all things, this resulted in thousands of people buying up millions of matches. Aunt Kate was one of those people. Proud of her quick action, she was not concerned that we now had enough matches to last years but more so happy with her prompt measures that would ensure we would not be ill effected. There was no way she wanted our lives to suffer inconvenience and she was adamant that no war would remove our creature comforts.

In early June 1942, Sydney residents were stunned as the war with Japan reached our doorsteps. The threat of invasion was very real as three Japanese midget submarines "suicide craft" attacked Sydney Harbour. As at Pearl Harbour, the Japanese chose the weekend, being least expected on a Sunday evening. Rainstorms had swept the coast on Sunday afternoon and it was suggested that these conditions might have offered the opportunity sought by the enemy to creep in for the launching of this most daring attack. Entering Port Jackson, one of the raiders was destroyed by gunfire while the other two were finally put out of action by depth charges.

Gunfire was heard echoing across the water, at intervals throughout the night and despite the advantage of surprise the only damage done by the enemy was the sinking of a small non-combatant craft "The Kuttabul" at its moorings. The audacity of the Japanese, in such attacks was recognised as characteristic and the event no less daring than any of those recorded anywhere. Within the newspapers, details of the attack were reported.

"Any lingering popular belief in Southern Australia that "it can not happen here" should now be completely dispelled. The risks under which Australians live belong no more to the realm of theory, nor can official warnings be regarded merely as disciplinary exhortations, for the enemy has come in person to announce them in unmistakable form."

People gathered in groups, discussing the latest events. For many, the attack on Sydney was a rude reminder that the war posed a serious threat to their liberty and the threat of invasion was real. In a recorded message, by National Stations our Prime Minister Mr. Curtin said:*"The threat of invasions hangs over us hourly, just as surely as the early pioneers daily apprehended the threat of thirst, of starvation, of death at the hands of the blacks and other dangers that beset a small and isolated community. Stand fast together as Australians. The heritage won by our forefathers is ours. We are now called on to hold it."*

Aunt Kate was horrified by the closeness of the war; I began to see the fear creeping into her expressions. Although, she constantly assured me we would both remain safe from harm. I could sense a trembling in her voice and so I tried in earnest to block out all negative thoughts. Reading the newspapers, it was evident that nearly every person in the world was effected. I was fortunate in my situation. Unlike many, I never went without food; I had shelter and all the comforts I could want for. No close friends or relatives were fighting on the war fronts. Worry engulfed so many people, for them there was no escaping while loved ones were missing or off fighting. Patiently, they would wait for news, for many, news only bought further devastation as reports of casualties and deaths were received. The strain of wartime conditions and the absence of loved ones certainly took their toll. Many suffered nervous breakdowns and had to relinquish their employment. Others found themselves residing in charity shelters such as the Salvation Army Homes.

To me, it appeared there would be no ending. The war had been going on for years, for years we had heard of the allied advances, of great defeats yet still, the fighting continued. Would there ever be peace?

In August 1942, sugar was added to the ration list. Every Australian citizen was allocated one pound or about half a kilo per week. It was no bed of roses, especially for women and families with growing children, placing pressure on those with a sweet tooth, who enjoyed sweets, jams and puddings.

As the war continued, rationing expanded to include other essentials such as butter, that had its allowance reduced over time resulting in bitter complaints. Meat was also included, as the government intended to export meat to the United Kingdom. Unlike previous items, rationed meat was a more complicated affair. Two pounds or about one kilo per week was the allocated allowance per person; this applied to lamb, mutton, veal and beef. Fish and poultry did not classify as meat, sausages were made of many different kinds of meat while rabbits and the off cuts went coupon free.

Other items that were rationed included rice, potatoes, margarine, coffee, prunes and many fresh fruits and vegetables. People were encouraged to be as self sufficient as possible, to grow their own vegetables and to keep hens for eggs. Some public parks underwent amazing transformations, air raid shelters sat securely next to communal vegetable gardens. Shortages and rationing resulted in hoarding; items in demand were sold privately at very high prices. A black market was created outside the rationing system. Aunt Kate continued to assure me that no war would disrupt us. She was a woman of great determination. I felt safe when she was nearby. I was also well aware of the underhanded dealings she conducted, even with the sly grog trade.

As I sit here and type away, I find myself chuckling as I just recalled an incident that may help you understand how much determination Aunt Kate possessed. This incident occurred not long after I moved in with Aunt Kate. Therefore, I was still reasonably young, at that stage in life where things made me laugh and scream at the same time and where I loved excitement but hated embarrassment. Anyway, Aunt Kate, Stella and I had decided to take a day trip to Parramatta for a picnic. There was a great picnic area at the end of Sutherland Road, which is now known as Silverwater Road. In those days, no bridge crossed the Parramatta River; Sutherland Road ended on the banks. This was a great place for locals and a like to relax and enjoy the outdoors, you were able to hire boats from the boat shed and swim in the tidal pool that was next to the wharf.

At the time, Aunt Kate owned a 1937 Hudson Straight Eight. How remember that car with its shiny teal paint, white walled tyres, its classy sideboard that ran between the back and front wheel guards and the delicately placed dual side mounted spares with hard covers. Being driven around in it, I felt like royalty with its interior of drawing room luxury, ample leg space, large comfy seats, shiny dashboard, internal lights and comfortable arm rests. I was the envy of so many.

Well on this particular day, we had all enjoyed a nice sleep in, followed by a big breakfast of scrambled eggs and toast with copious cups of tea to wash it all down. Once finished, we cleaned up the breakfast dishes before packing a picnic basket. Fresh chicken sandwiches, jam tarts Stella had baked the previous evening, a selection of fruit and a bottle of lime flavoured Cottee's cordial. Along with the clothes we were wearing, we also packed our bathers and some towels. With our intention to go for a relaxing stroll and swim to build our appetites before indulging in our picnic food. It was a beautiful day outside with not a cloud in the sky.

Travelling along Parramatta Road the mood was high, as we discussed recent events and sang a variety of songs. However, approaching the Liverpool Road turn off near Ashfield I was beginning to experience the effects of my tea drinking and could feel my bulging bladder stretch every time we hit a bump in the road. Biting down on my lip, I started to sweat and began to fidget, realising I would not make it to the river. Feeling desperate to relieve this pressure, I held my stomach and lent forward asking Aunt Kate if she could find a lavatory. Luckily, relief came quickly as Aunt Kate stopped the car on Parramatta Road in front of Ashfield Park and I made a dash into the local bowling club. Aunt Kate and Stella greeted me as I exited the club. Together we stretched our legs, walking across the grass in Ashfield Park down to the rotunda that had once stood at Farm Cove before strolling back along to the George and Mary Watson Fountain then to the car.

All was perfect, well that is until we got back into the car. Starting the engine, Aunt Kate attempted to place the car into gear, the only problem being it was stuck in reverse. And that was where the fun began.

After about five minutes of struggling with the gears to no avail, Aunt Kate declared, "We are going to have our picnic on the river, come hell or high water and no motorcar is going to stop us." With that she placed her foot on the accelerator and we were on our way, all be it still in reverse heading straight across to the other side of Parramatta Road. From the back seat I let out a god almighty scream and Aunt Kate snapped, "Keep quiet Shirley, you will draw attention to us." I was in shock. We were on the wrong side of the road. Her car was pointing towards Sydney, yet travelling in reverse we were heading towards Parramatta and there she was worried I would be the one to draw attention to us. Placing her foot on the brake, the car came to a sudden stand still and she instructed Stella to climb into the back.

"You are both going to have to help me watch out for other cars," she said firmly.

I could not believe it was really happening. We were still about eight miles or just under thirteen kilometres away from the picnic grounds. Normally, when driving forward it would still take another half-hour, in this predicament most people would have just abandoned the idea, but not Aunt Kate. Stella was laughing and shaking her head.

"You are really going to do this aren't you Miss Indy," she said as she jumped into the back seat. Aunt Kate responded with one simple word, "Yes!"

With her right hand firmly placed on the steering wheel, her left arm slung over the front seat. And her body twisted so that she could look over her left shoulder, we were all set and once again on our way. Stella and I spent the rest of the trip perched up on our knees looking out the back window. We had front row seats in this escapade, ducking and weaving in response to Aunt Kate's cries. The entire trip was spent cheering, laughing and bellowing out warnings. Successfully, weaving around the obstacles of cars parked next to the gutter, turning corners and manoeuvring through intersections. Thank goodness, we also went undetected by the law. Mind you, we did receive numerous strange looks along the way. Nevertheless, that didn't deter Aunt Kate, as I say she was definitely a woman of great determination.

Arriving at the park, the car came to a stand still and Aunt Kate turned the engine off, at which time Stella exclaimed, "I think I need a drink!" well that just resulted in raptures of laughter. I am not sure if it was due to our comical experience or relief that we had finally made it safe and well, I suspect it was probably both.

With our picnic a success, we opted leave the car there and travel home by train. Needless to say, when we finally made it home Aunt Kate was straight on the phone to the car sales manager. And after a brief exchange of some very diplomatic abuse she hung up, advising they were to have the car repaired and returned without delay. In the meantime, she should expect to see a temporary vehicle delivered by lunchtime the following day. Aunt Kate rarely swore nor raised her voice, but was more than capable of putting a case forward and being very persuasive with her requests. Persuasive, determined, protective and yes at times underhanded.

I never let on that I was aware of her underhanded dealings, especially throughout the period of rationing, but was truly thankful for her actions and my comfortable lifestyle. With the war continuing, I wanted to offer assistance and so I visited the local Salvation Army lodgings and asked what I could do. I was only young and could not offer much, but was sure any offer would not go astray. They welcomed my offer and so my volunteer work commenced. Every Saturday, I would visit there and assist in the preparation of meals, which would feed the less fortunate. For many, these meals were the only ones they could afford. I had also acquired a job at a local department store; this employment gave me a feeling of worth. Aunt Kate was happy to see me up early every morning; she was glad that I was continuing with my life like many of my own age. I was eighteen, now a young woman and it was time that I started to contribute to the financial side of my life.

Work was not as I had imagined. For so long, when I was younger I had dreamed of having financial independence. However, when I commenced employment, all I wished for was that I could return to the ways I had experienced while at school. I never realised that along with work was also a responsibility to my employer. School had previously felt like a chore, only when I commenced work did I realise how much fun school really was. Yes, there were rules and homework, but there was never the worry of having to answer to a boss. My boss Mr. Evans was stricter than any school teacher I had encountered, the young girl who worked in my position previously, had been sacked as her cash register did not balance. This behaviour regardless as to whether it was accidental was not tolerated neither was untidiness nor lateness.

I was on my feet nearly all day, by the time I made it home I was relieved to remove my shoes and happy to relax in a hot bath. I remember when I first started employment; my legs gave me so much pain I feared they were going to drop off, while both heels were covered in Band-Aids hiding blisters. I was in agony everyday, but never the less, I put on a happy face and served the customers with all the fine pleasantries they expected. After three months of probation, I was authorised to balance the cash register. Mr. Evans was pleased with my progress and very happy with the compliments he received regarding the service I provided. *The Customer is always right and must come first* was his motto. As shop assistants, it was our duty to offer the customer everything that would keep them happy and see them returning for further sales. Aunt Kate would help me where possible; at parties she would tell all her friends of my job and instruct them to pay me a visit. They were people who could afford new clothes and had the ability to obtained the required coupons regardless of the times. Their visits impressed Mr. Evans, especially when they waved their money around and insisted on being served by me.

I recall one morning when Norma paid the store a visit; head stuck high in the air. She made a point of making her way to Mr. Evans. He could tell that she was a woman of money, her fingers were covered in gold, her shoulders covered by a fur. Mr. Evans hurriedly approached advising her that he was the store manager and would be only too happy to offer his personal service. However, his mouth soon dropped wide open as his offer was rejected with Norma promptly responding by telling him that there was only one young lady who she would be happy with. Norma certainly had a way with words and knew exactly how to make people feel insignificant. I had never seen anyone dare to put Mr. Evans in his place and found the whole scene amusing as I watched and listened from a distance. Giving a full account of how his store had been highly recommended to her by her friends due to the fabulous service they had received and not wanting to let on that she was a friend Norma gave Mr. Evans my description and insisted he take her to me.

Keeping myself composed as they approached, I straightened the counter and when they finally made it to me, I put on my happy face and greeted them both with an enthusiastic and very cheery, "Good Morning." Norma winked at me without Mr. Evans seeing, then instructed him that she no longer required his services. Within one hour, she purchased four pairs of shoes, one evening dress, six pairs of stockings, two lace handkerchiefs, three scarfs' and one jacket. It was the biggest individual sale our store had made in months, required coupons accompanied her cash payment and Norma departed bags in hand. Mr. Evans was more than just a little impressed with my sales abilities. Norma was pleased with her amusement and shopping and I received an early mark as we reached our reduced daily sales quota plus a bonus in my weekly pay for my hard work. All in all, I would have to classify that day at the store as one of my most satisfying. I knew Norma had the money to spend. I knew she could get her hands on what ever coupons she needed, she was there simply to fill in her time and she would delight in buying what ever took her fancy. When she was at Aunt Kate's I would always ensure her glass was topped up, this little adventure was merely a demonstration of her gratitude.

Aunt Kate burst into laughter when I told her of the episode. She could easily imagine the antics Norma would have displayed, knowing only too well the attitude she was capable of demonstrating.

CHAPTER TWELVE

1945, A mushroom cloud rose above Hiroshima as the first atomic bomb was dropped. With detonation, nearly one hundred and thirty thousand lives were lost and the war was nearly over. It was by far the greatest war of all time; three quarters of the world's population took part. More than six million indirect victims had died in Nazi concentration camps. Either worked to death, shot, gassed or given lethal injections. Others died of starvation or as a result of experiments performed on them by the Nazi scientists and doctors. It was an atrocity of all atrocities. Total human cost - over sixty million with twenty-five million military and a further thirty million civilians.

That was the topic of discussion at my twenty-first, not what you would consider normal these days. The war had just ended and although Australia was half way around the world from where most of the horror occurred, we did not go unscathed. Anti-Nazi protesters could be heard in the streets, mostly found outside businesses owned by Germans who had settled within Australia long before the war commenced. These Germans, were innocent victims of racist abuse; many were rounded up and imprisoned in internment camps - supervised by the military.

For people of German origin, living in Australia became very difficult. To say you felt sorry for these innocent victims, in many instances landed you in an argument. For many Australians, fear had turned into anger as loved ones left our shores to fight in a war they never started. Many never returned.

I recalled quite clearly the day a friend of mine, Petra Schultz, was taunted by local children. The name calling quickly turned nasty, as stones were thrown smashing the front windows of her house. An innocent German girl, only twenty years of age, who had lived in Australia for most of her life. Yet, the war, so many miles away cost her many friends and her job. There were no anti-discrimination boards in those days to protect workers.

Petra was out of work and alone with her unemployed mother. Her father had been taken to an internment camp, south west of Sydney. I could not understand the cruelty, which was being inflicted upon so many innocent individuals just because of their heritage. I could not understand many of the events, that were taking place within the world. Intense hatred for our civilisation, which had permitted such atrocities would at times overwhelm me; my faith in mankind had been shattered over the proceeding years.

Aunt Kate, my loving aunt Kate also felt lost within the violence and anger. She agreed that we could assist my childhood friend Petra and her mother. Without us, I don't know how they would have survived. Employed by Aunt Kate to do housework, they would cook, clean and sew and in return, food and safe lodgings were provided. I recall it taking some convincing Mrs. Shultz that she was not a charity case or an individual rejected by the entire nation but valued assistance we required. She was a woman of great pride and her pride had to be cast aside for the sake of survival. I thought by helping them, I could make up for the wrong I had committed within my life. I thought by doing good, my guilt would be eased - it was not.

After the duration of the war, Petra's father was released and he returned home to Paddington. His stay, only long enough to settle financial matters and pack the family possessions. No longer comfortable with the Sydney surroundings, due to the ill feeling that had been created in the time of war, they moved to Melbourne to again start a new life.I sometimes wondered what ever became of the Schultz family. I hoped they were able to find peace in their new city.

My twenty-first birthday was celebrated with mixed feelings; I was a bag of mixed emotions, happiness and relief the war was over and joy that I had made it this far. I was a young woman, working as a shop assistant in a major department store. Not exactly, the position I had envisaged, but no less it was a job and that was something to be grateful for.

Many of my peers remained out of work; employment was still difficult to find especially if you were a female. Others, were called up for labour force work in food canneries. Positions that created feelings of hostility and resentment. Their freedom of choice had been stolen by the manpower authorities that were in charge of deploying a work force in the best interest of the war. I was one of the lucky ones.

Six years had passed since my parents' disappearance; the police file was now stamped as unsolved. It was on my twenty-first that I legally took ownership of our family home at Paddington. It was also on my twenty-first that I inherited my parent's savings. I was twenty-one and I would never have to endure the financial struggles so many around me would.

Aunt Kate hosted my party and I was surrounded by many whom loved and cared for me. Yet, I also experienced a feeling of great loss and emptiness. My parents were no longer here. My one true friend and love, Bugsy was gone.

I was not sure if I was ready for such a large change, my aunt said, "You can stay with me for as long as you wish." It was a genuine offer and I accepted. My family home at Paddington had remained vacant since my parents' disappearance, boarded up from the inside to prevent squatters getting in. The once manicured lawns, now only received the occasional trim and weeds had suffocated the flowering garden beds over time. The priority of maintaining such show stopping large gardens had disappeared along with my parents. In the months that had followed their disappearance, Aunt Kate had instructed her gardener to complete a monthly lawn mowing. Advising him, the only purpose in his role was in deterring unwanted guests, by making it look reasonable so as passers by would think someone lived inside. The gum tree, which my father had lopped some twelve years prior had recovered and grown to a tall height.

They say, a person's home is where their heart is, for me it was with Aunt Kate in her house. Our love and acceptance for each other was reciprocated. Her lifestyle was not one which could be referred to as normal and neither was mine. I was very selective in choosing friends and I made every attempt to keep people at an arms length. Even at my twenty-first birthday, guests mainly consisted of family members with a handful of friends. People I had studied with throughout my school years and one colleague I shared my lunch break with at work. Aunt Kate being a professional artist met many people, her circle of friends included numerous socialites, the rich and famous. She was an extrovert, and for that period she was very open and forward thinking. Unlike my mother, who was one to sit back in the shadow of my father, Aunt Kate needed no one to over-shadow her. She was a straight up and down person, what you saw was what you got. That was something I admired; her strength to face the world. If I could only be half the person she was, I would be more than just content.

She had the ability to do more than just listen to what people said. She would hear their words. She would feel their emotions, she was a people person and I was not. I am sure that is why she never hesitated to help anyone she could. She was a spiritual person, not a Catholic or Protestant, but a person who believed in karma.

What goes around comes around. All good things come to those who wait. Treat everyone as you would like to be treated yourself. Three statements she used on many occasions. I would sit and listen to her, hoping I would never suffer for my wrongdoing. I wondered if the karma was only received for, those acts committed after you passed a certain age. How is it a young person could be punished later in life, for an act that was committed when they were younger, when they lacked understanding?

My birthday celebrations went into the early hours of the morning. After a few too many bubblies, I said my goodnights and retreated to my bedroom upstairs. Lying on my bed I could hear the chatter downstairs, the laughter and jokes continued. My bed was spinning and in an attempt to stop this feeling, I placed my foot over the edge of my bed until it gently touched the floor and I passed out.

CHAPTER THIRTEEN

Isn't it terrible, when you wake after having a few too many drinks the night before and you still feel as though you are intoxicated. That was how I felt the day after my birthday. As I made my way downstairs I struggled to inhale deeply, thinking it would assist in my settling, however, I only felt my head spin. The sofa was my best bet, so I flopped onto it. Lowering my head, I wiped both eyes with the palms of my hands, trying to clear the blurry vision. I yawned and scanned the lounge room. My birthday cake or what remained of it was sitting on the dining table. Empty bottles of champagne stacked beside it, along with half empty glasses. I stretched upwards, yawning again while lowering my hands to my head. My left hand resting there as my right moved down the back of my head and around the back of my neck. Reclining back on the sofa, I again inhaled deeply, held my breath and let out a loud sigh.

"Good morning," came a voice from behind. It was my Aunt Kate's friend Stella. Obviously, she had stayed the night, she too was an artist and along with Kate, they certainly knew how to consume large amounts of bubbly. At times, I tried to work out who was the greatest influence, but generally, I could not decide. Both enjoyed living life to the fullest, both influenced each other.

She was wearing one of my aunts' shirts and from the sunlight, which shone behind her, it did not appear anything else. The lines of her well-rounded hips and small waist were visible through the sheer material. After studying her standing there for a while, I replied, "Good morning." She approached me from behind and placed her soft and caring hands on my shoulders.

"Great Party, you should turn twenty-one more often." Her hands were now massaging my neck. It was the first time in a long while since I had been touched. The first time I had ever been touched in that way by a woman. I liked it; she had soft and caring hands. Hands, which made me feel comfortable in what, I would normally consider an intrusive situation.

Aunt Kate made an entrance from down the stairs; she too looked a little worse for wear. Stella removed her hands and offered to make some coffee. In an instant, she was gone, into the kitchen followed by Aunt Kate.

For the rest of the day, I lounged around, too hungover and unable to exert any energy.

The war was over and everyone could relax, tension which had filled the air for so many years was beginning to disappear. Not only was everyone celebrating my birthday, they were also celebrating freedom. I sat on the sofa recalling incidences from the previous night.

There had been so much jubilation, people were up dancing to Jazz; The Original Dixieland Jazz Band, The Great Louis Armstrong and how could I ever forget the wonderful voice of Ella Fitzgerald.

Aunt Margaret and Uncle Tom had also been at the party for a while; I hadn't seen them or at least my aunt since the previous Christmas. She never changed, a typical housewife, she reminded me of my mother. I was sure as they left, she was thinking about what she could prepare for my uncle's dinner; wanting to please her husband.

My grandma Edna was also there, she appeared

uncomfortable within her surroundings, when outside her home in Faulconbridge she instantly transformed into a quiet woman of very few words. A stark contrast to her daughter Kate. Grandma Edna sat quiet on the lounge for most of the night; she stayed only until my birthday cake was cut. I recall sitting on the other side of the room watching her, at times, I felt sorry for her. My grandfather had passed away when I was only young, accidentally shot while shooting rabbits. Although, I did not have any clear recollection of him being in my life, I wondered if my grandmother missed him. I also wondered if she missed her son, my father. She had never asked me how I felt about my parent's disappearance. She never asked how I was coping and to me she really did not seem to care.

Aunt Kate's house was immaculate, yet my grandmother dared not touch anything, her eyes wandered around the room.Every now and again, her eyes would meet with another person and she would give a half smile, still not saying a word. Then, when eye contact was detached the sombre look would return to her face once more.

I had lived with Aunt Kate for six years, by that stage. In that entire time, Grandma only visited twice. Initially, on the first anniversary of my parent's disappearance. The second time, for our family Christmas dinner in 1943. Aunt Kate insisted on the dinner being at her house. She set out all her fine china and silverware. It was a lovely day out on the lawn. Everyone chatting away, telling his or her latest tales, yet Grandma again sat still on her chair with a sombre look displayed on her face. It was as if being at Aunt Kate's house caused her grief. Kate was different to the rest of her family and my grandma did not seem to accept her. I was sure that she loved Kate, it was just the acceptance of her individualism that she denied. Maybe, it was just the way she had been raised, not a lot of hugging went on in those days, the word love was almost a four letter word like others as far as the older generation was concerned. I never saw them embrace and that was strange. Aunt Kate was a huggable kind of person and she embraced life and everyone she met. Yet, it was as if a huge force field stood between them preventing them from ever achieving closeness.

I was always taught to respect my elders, but I often questioned this instruction. My theory was that you should respect those who respect you. Respect - refrain from violating, to honour, to value, to heed. How can a person respect others who do not in turn, respect them as individuals. I did love my grandma, however, her attitude towards Aunt Kate did not go unnoticed and I could not show her the respect most grandchildren showed their grandparents.

My grandma had lived through two wars, yet this was no excuse for her attitude. Aunt Kate was in many ways outrageous in her behaviour, especially for those conservative times, but she was her daughter and if Aunt Kate could love unconditionally then my grandma should have been able to have those same capabilities.

Sometimes, her attitude would infuriate me; I wanted to know why she had such a problem in accepting Aunt Kate as an individual. Respect, bloody hell, she had to accept people for who they were, only then could she learn how to respect. Only then, would she get the respect she thought she was entitled to.

CHAPTER FOURTEEN

My grandma Edna died in 1949, I always knew she would make old bones, but for some reason, I never told her that I loved her and this I did regret. I also never asked her why she did not accept Aunt Kate as an individual. Ding-dong the old bitch has gone, was the first thought that crossed my mind at the news of her passing.

There were five of us at her funeral, which was held at Leura in the Blue Mountains, Aunt Kate, Stella, Aunt Margaret and Uncle Tom and me. While the passing of someone is generally considered a sad time, not a tear was shed. For me, the sad part was the dismal attendance and the lack of emotion. Without Gran, I would not exist. Or would I? Would I have been born into another family, maybe into another time? These were the thoughts that travelled through my mind, as I watch her coffin disappear below the surface of the earth.

Shortly after Gran's funeral, Aunt Kate asked me if I could spare a Saturday night, as she had wished to discuss some things with me. I was nearing twenty-five at the time and had lived with her for nearly ten years. Maybe, she wanted to reclaim her house as her own. Although at this stage I was also extremely independent and spent a lot of my free time out and about maybe I had out worn my welcome.

Accepting her request, I cancelled my plans for the next Saturday night's dance and nervously waited.

Finally, Saturday night arrived and as we sat down to dinner, Aunt Kate began our discussion.

"Shirley, I do enjoy you living here but..." she paused.

"Yes Kate, what?" immediately I feared what she would say next.

"What do you want out of life Shirley? You go to work, you come home, you have friends but I have never really seen you with any boys."

Again she paused, looking for answers I could not give.

Shrugging my shoulders, I struggled to find some words, however, before I had the chance she continued.

"I am worried that you holding back on living your life to its fullest potential. You attend engagements, then weddings. You celebrate in your friends happiness when they announce themselves as being pregnant then celebrate more when they hold their little bundles of joy. But what about your life?"

Sitting there, I smiled as I thought briefly about some of the events I had experienced. Nothing gave me more joy than being able to share in the experience of my friend's happiness. However, was she right? After all, it was not my happiness and my biological clock was ticking. Most women had already started creating families by there mid twenties, while I appeared to be sitting on the sidelines. Had I been sabotaging my ability to find love, by holding onto the memories of Bugsy? Was it even possible, that over time I had embellished Bugsy thus creating an unrealistic image of the man who would fulfil my dreams? I had met many men throughout the years. Yet, none compared to Bugsy. Was it really Bugsy I compared them to or the glorified memory of a young man, who I had once greatly admired, that had now been placed high upon a pedestal within my mind?

"Of course I want a family, I just haven't met the right man!" I declared.

"I didn't mean to upset you Shirley, you know I want you to be happy, I want what is best for you."

"Okay, maybe I am just fussy, you know me, but hey, you never know that perfect man may be right around the corner."

Leaning over, I reached out and hugged Aunt Kate, reassuring her all would be fine. I knew she wanted what was best for me, but still, there was no way that I would settle for someone who I thought was second best.

The 1950's, was a time where young males were referred to as Bodgies, while the females were called Widgies. Alarmists expressed concerns that these teenagers were becoming delinquent and uncontrollable congregating in milk bars and on street corners.They listened to all the "wrong" music including Elvis, although these days their behaviour would not be considered rebellious but back then it was shocking.

I thought it was great to see those younger than I take charge of their lives. Australia was rapidly changing and opening up to a greater number of worldly influences from all directions, including both the cinema and music. After the war ended, many countries had experienced a refugee crisis. Shiploads of immigrants flooded Australians shores, wanting to build a new life. "Wog" the slang term used to describe those immigrants from Middle Eastern and European origin such as Greeks, Germans and Italians was created. Unlike the crappy immigration policy Australia appears to have adapted these days, the 1950's was an era of "assimilation" where migrants were expected to abandon their culture and language and "blend in" with the existing population.

I loved the 1950's, I loved my new "wog" friends and we enjoyed going to the beach together. Munching down on piping hot fish and chips, purchased from the corner store, delicately wrapped in old newspaper. With the increasing population, came an increasing number of restaurant experiences. Chinese food was popular and while some restaurants displayed traditional foods such as chips and baked beans in an attempt to draw in customers, I wanted the complete Chinese experience.

Coogee Beach, replaced my once loved Bondi Beach in summer. It was renowned for its board riders, those bronzed Aussie lifeguards, children playing, sand castles, ice creams and sun lotion. Coogee was the place to be, it even had the occasional shark scare to keep everyone on his or her toes. Nothing was better than going on a picnic or to the beach and being surrounded by great friends; towels scattered closely together while sun baking and eating hot chips laced with vinegar followed by ice creams. The 1950's represented casual living and Saturday night dances were a place to meet people.

The Stones Cabaret, in Coogee was an amazing place in its day. It was also the place I first laid my eyes on Johnny O'Keefe. The year was 1956 and I still had no man in my life, but this year would see two huge events, television arrived in Australia and I was introduced to Australia's King of Rock 'n' Roll, Johnny O'Keefe. Johnny was a member of "The Dee Jays." He was stocky in build and pretty average in appearance, but when it came to his performances, I was wowed. Standing up on stage wearing his brightly coloured suits, gold lame jackets and suits with fur trims, he would caress the microphone in such suggestive manners that he would make me go weak at the knees. He was dynamic and electrifying. He was like Elvis but only better, as Elvis was far away on the other side of the world, while Johnny strut his stuff right before my very eyes. Johnny was the man of my dreams, far less of a handful than many of my friend's men. I could dream all I liked, see him perform and then return to my own existence. I was not ready for the constriction of marriage. Life was fun just as it was and with Johnny skyrocketing to fame and releasing hit after hit, I could turn him on and off when ever I chose.

In March 1958, Johnny released "Wild One" a song that in part I believed reflected my attitude towards life. I was maybe a tad older than most others who enjoyed Rock 'n' Roll but Rock 'n' Roll was here, life was to be lived and there was definitely no time for settling down. I no longer cared what people thought about my not marrying. Life was too short and had to be enjoyed.Rock music dominated my life and moves on the dance floor like jive kept me fit and feeling young at heart.

I miss the good old days, all the dancing and just having clean fun.

Time was passing by at an amazing rate; I didn't want to blink fearing I would miss something. By 1959 Australia's population hit ten million, by 1960 the Opera House with its eccentric roof was starting to take shape. Everything I could ever want was right at my doorstep, Australia was the place to be and we even had a visit from the Queen in 1954.

Australia offered so many opportunities and I wanted to be a part of everything, restriction free, the world was my oyster. I had a carefree life. That was until…

In late November 1961, no one felt safe walking the Sydney streets at night.Headlines of daily newspapers read, "Mutilator Strikes Again." A serial killer was on the loose, a homicidal madman, a psychopath.

On 4th June 1961, police had been summoned to the Domain Baths in Sydney. A man's nude corpse had been found, savagely attacked, stabbed over thirty times and mutilated. Then on 21st November a second body was discovered and police were summoned to a public toilet in Moore Park, just a stone throw from where we lived. This time the victim had his throat slashed, was covered in blood and riddled with puncture wounds, after being stabbed about fifty times. Like the previous victim, his body had been mutilated in a violent frenzy.

The thought of walking home after work terrified me, after seeing the newspaper headlines. I had completed the same walk nearly all my working life and yet, from then on it was no longer a casual affair, I was more than a little dubious. On the day of seeing the headlines, I made certain to finish work right on five o'clock although the daylight would be shining for still a couple of hours. There was no way I wanted to chance a meeting with a madman.

My journey was generally a casual stroll, which took about forty-five minutes. That night, my pace quickened and I made it home within half an hour. Entering the front door, I sighed in relief, I had worked up a sweat and Aunt Kate came to my side concerned something may be wrong.After assuring her that everything was fine, I went to the kitchen and poured us a scotch. I needed a drink to settle my nerves, a murderer was on the loose, no one knew his identity and I was sure I did not want to cross the path of a murderer.

That night, I made sure all the doors were locked, not that the murderer had claimed any victims in their houses yet, but I had to be sure that I felt safe. I even went around the house to make sure the windows were also locked. All my concern put Aunt Kate on edge, she assured me that no murderer would ever step foot in her house. Her assurances could not ease my worry and I did not sleep very well that night.

For the next couple of months, I remained on edge, only venturing out in the dark when necessary. On Australia Day 1962 I attended a function at a colleague's house in nearby Randwick. By that time, my fear of this unknown serial killer was all but forgotten. After a big day of celebrations and a few too many drinks, I decided it was time to venture home. At about nine o'clock I gathered my coat and set off across Centennial Park. It was not until I made my way deep into the dimly lit parkland that I began to have doubts regarding my safety.

Approaching me was the figure of a man, in his hand he held an unidentifiable object. My mind boggled. Could it be a knife? Was I to be the victim of a ferocious attack? I could feel my heart beating. The figure slipped into the shadows. My pupils dilated, as I strained to make out the object within his hands, which every now and again flickered as its shiny surface met with the moonlight. My ears pricked, listening to every sound as the grass crumpled below my feet. I was in sensory over-drive.

Finally, the figure emerged from the shadows; he did not appear to have the characteristics of a murderer. Very well presented in a suit and in his hand he carried a silver pen. As he walked, he tossed the pen in the air catching it, then throwing it up in the air again. As our paths met, he threw the pen once more; however, this time he dropped it and from the expression on his face, he appeared a little embarrassed.

"Evening to you," he remarked as he bent for the

pen. I too bent to the ground, attempting to retrieve his pen and with our bending, heads collided. All the tension that had surrounded me only a moment before was gone, replaced by laughter, which echoed through the park.

After our laughter subsided, he introduced himself as Edward Rutherford; taking my hand he raised it to his mouth and kissed it.

"It is a pleasure to meet such a lovely young lady in such a beautiful place."

I blushed; it had been a long time since I had received such a wonderful compliment. Lost for words, I stood before him with a smile from ear to ear, "Thank you," I replied. After my reply, Edward continued talking, he asked if he might have my telephone number. Then he said, "If it does not seem too presumptuous of me I would like it very much if I may one day have the pleasure of your company at dinner." His words were very well spoken and I could not resist such an invitation. I nodded and handed him my telephone number. After which, we parted company and I continued my walk back to Aunt Kate's. An unusual encounter and a bizarre reaction to a stranger.

Early the next morning, I received a telephone call. It was Edward Rutherford. Just as he had been the night before in our strange encounter, his words were very fluent and polite. He assured me that he did not make a habit of picking up young ladies within a dimly lit Centennial Park and invited me out for dinner on the following Saturday night. An invitation I eagerly accepted.

Saturday night could not come around soon enough, the excitement I felt surprised me. I felt, as though I was a child once more waiting for Christmas morning, wondering what presents I would receive. Finally, the doorbell rang. I felt butterflies. I was thirty-seven years old and normally I should have been over the nerves of dating. Yet, I was not, this was the first time I had had a date. As the evening progressed my nerves quickly disappeared and I realised, Edward was the first man I felt comfortable with in a long time.

The night was a success; Edward was both handsome and charming. As I looked at him from the other side of the table, I thought of Bugsy. I wondered if Bugsy might have turned out the same as Edward had he been alive. For me, it was love at first sight with Edward. He was the man of my dreams, the type of man who up until only a week ago, I could dream about. I felt I should pinch myself just to make sure he was more than a figment of my imagination. I did. The pinch hurt and he was no figment, he was real.

I wanted to know everything about him and so I ask him to tell me every little detail of his life. Over dinner I learned much of Edward's past. Previously, he had only been involved in two relationships. The first, was with a beautiful woman. They had met in their younger years and had supported each other through very trying times. Unfortunately, he said as the years rolled by for him the relationship while secure and predictable appeared to stagnate and his feelings were more so that of friendship. As he spoke of his first love tears welled in his eyes. I could see that he was sincere in his words as he described his separation and the hurting this woman, Angela as one of the biggest regrets in his life.

His second relationship, at first appeared to be in stark contrast to the previous one. Julie worked within his office. She was boisterous and full of spontaneity; she offered Edward the excitement he thought his life had lacked. This however, he explained was short lived, while the lovely Julie said in one breath that she loved him she was also expressing great interest in many others, accepting telephone numbers and flirting at every chance she had. Her secrets being revealed after confrontations about overheard telephone conversations, unexplained disappearances and notes found containing names and writings detailing numerous lies. Edward discovered her world was built on fantasies, bullshit and greed and was no longer able to determine what were facts or fiction. He no longer wished to take part in what he believed were her mind games and so he withdrew his interest from the relationship he could not escape. Finally, his inattention paid off and after a period of about eighteen months and seemingly bored, Julie demanded the relationship to be over. Accusing him of cheating, she immediately began belittling and bad-mouthing his name to all that would listen. Accusations flew thick and fast and Edward found himself having to defend his character, while she sat back trying to destroy it at every opportunity.

Edward described her as, "deranged and delusional." Within days of collecting some of her belongings she had left at his house she was seeing another man, telephoning Edward in an intoxicated state and asking him for sex or just wanting to know his every move. It was as if she had decided that she should move on with her life, yet, he was supposed to sit in a world of emptiness.

This harassment he said continued for months. Julie still had some of his belongings and refused to give them back, and initially Edward had insisted on wanting his possessions returned, it was a matter of principle. In the later months, after the separation he informed Julie that he had resigned himself to the fact he would never see his belongings and therefore she could do what ever she chose with the items. She had been using the knowledge of his wanting his things to keep the contact, trying to pull at his strings like a puppet and a puppet he was not. She was a materialistic person and enjoyed playing with emotions. At one stage, she even threatened to take half of the house in which he lived with his mother. Julie was aware Edward's name was on the title deeds but luckily for him she never had any legal hold over his share.

Hearing slanderous rumours which many claimed had originated from Julie he insisted she stop. However, she laughed and informed him these things were merely comments made as probes, so that she would know whom he was still talking to. She was a destructive individual, who it appeared would stop at nothing until she was ready. Maybe he thought the behaviour was the result of her being placed in a similar position as the one he found himself in. Maybe, the only thing that she possessed in her heart was revenge, she hadn't been able to seek revenge for her past failures and Edward had offered himself as an easy target. She appeared to love the idea of hurting, confusing and damaging another heart.

Finally, wanting the harassment to end and fearing it would not Edward went into seclusion, choosing to speak to no one, afraid Julie would learn of his movements and embark on another attack. His life consisted of work then home.

Ultimately, Julie gave up and resigned from work. Edward maintained a single lifestyle, finding enjoyment in his work and small circle of friends. Only now, had he found the courage to take the first step towards a relationship. Although he admitted at times he did miss the closeness of a relationship and the companionship he had not been prepared to open his heart to such, fearing a repeat of the Julie saga. Julie was a self absorbed manipulator, an outright bitch who took great delight in offending and crippling another persons esteem for her own sick self pleasure and amusement.

We continued dating and I felt a distinct joy returning to my life. Valentines Day soon arrived and I was showered in red roses. My world had taken a turn and this time it was for the better. I could feel a skip in my walk. The world appeared a better place. Although, I felt safe when I was with Edward, I always remained alert, being alone for such a long time can make an individual very wary of those around. I was used to my own company, the company of Aunt Kate and Stella but I was not used to the company of a man, especially one who spoke of me and to me with affection in his voice.

The June long weekend arrived and Edward asked if he may take me away for the weekend. Although, in my heart I would have loved to accept his invitation, my head told me that maybe things were going a little too fast. I declined his invitation and instead we stayed in Sydney.

I had not told Edward about the house I owned, which sat unoccupied in Paddington, all boarded up to prevent squatters. We had been dating for six months; however; I did not see it as necessary information. In the past, I had seen people put off by the possessions and or wealth of another. I did not want to chance this with Edward. If I told him of the house then he may have wanted to hear more about my past, about my parents and their whereabouts. I needed to have time to think, time to look within myself, to assess my feelings and so after the June weekend I asked if Edward would mind if we took things a little slower. Being the gentleman he was, he replied by telling me he would give me all the time I needed. He too, did not want to rush into anything and for me he would wait.

We continued seeing each other, although the dates were less frequent than before, this I enjoyed. I did have strong feelings for him; however, I also needed to have some space. I wanted nothing more than for our relationship to blossom and to last for what I considered was forever and a day plus more but jumping in without thinking clearly could jeopardise this dream.

By the time the first anniversary of our meeting rolled around, the intensity of my feelings had grown. I no longer had to go to sleep to dream. Edward was everything I had hoped for in a partner and so my thoughts turned to the idea of being married and starting a family.

In early August, Edward telephoned; his voice was not as cheery as it had been in the past. He explained to me that his employer had requested he transfer to their Melbourne office for an eighteen month assignment. Edward was torn; he was a loyal and dedicated worker whose ambition was to be promoted to a managerial position. This assignment would assist in his elevation; however, he was heartbroken at the thought of not seeing me for eighteen months. I assured Edward that I would wait for him, just as he had promised he would wait for me. And so, Edward accepted the transfer and left for Melbourne in early September 1963.

We continued to communicate, especially around Christmas, again I was showered in red roses. Even in his absence, my love for him grew more than I believed was ever possible, I could not explain the intense love I possessed towards him. At night, I would pray for his safe return. I would dream of our re-uniting and our future together.

CHAPTER FIFTEEN

2⁹ᵗʰ June 1964 - Stella gasped for breath, her facial expression was frozen in a state of shock and devastation. Aunt Kate and Stella had been very close for years, even long before I had moved in with Aunt Kate. Slowly she raised her hands, while closing her eyes and lowering her head, she only said one word, "Why?"

Her reaction to my news of Aunt Kate's death was worse than I had anticipated. I reached out for her and embraced her within my arms. Tears streamed down her cheeks, as she burst into uncontrollable wailing. Tears were also flowing from my eyes, as I stood still in the silence, my arms tightly around her tiny waist. After a few minutes, I slowly motioned her towards the sofa where we finally found rest. Echoes of sobbing and sniffles could be heard around the room, and so for what appeared to be hours, we sat still on the sofa within our tight embrace, a loved one had left us.

Aunt Kate was only fifty-three; they say only the good die young and that saying certainly applied to Aunt Kate. It was only weeks before that we all celebrated Stella's birthday together, never in our wildest dreams could we have imagined such a sudden and drastic loss. Aunt Kate had always appeared fit and healthy, she looked after herself, eating a healthy diet and exercising on a regular basis. She had been complaining about chest pains but when I questioned her she put them down to indigestion and from the raking of leaves she had been doing, stating that the pain would soon pass. I too was devastated and furious that I had not insisted she seek medical attention. Had she done this, they may have been able to detect an issue with her heart. There were so many people that really didn't deserve to be alive, so many people alive that simply would not be missed. Aunt Kate was not one of these people, she deserved to be alive and she would be missed, she was at the peak of her life and she had not harmed a soul.

First my parents, then Bugsy, then my grandma and now Aunt Kate. I was only thirty-nine and yet already in my life, I had seen and heard of so many atrocities, I had experienced the world at its worst. If there is a greater being, a God which people look up to, then how could he with all his power permit such things to occur?

Finally, Stella released herself from my embrace and rose from the sofa. Her eyes were puffy from crying and still displayed a blank look. She was in shock, she closed her eyes tightly as if she was praying that upon their opening this terrible news would vanish, that Aunt Kate would be standing in the room with us. However, that was not to be, Aunt Kate was gone forever.

The next few days were taken up by funeral arrangements; it was the first time I had arranged such a sad event. I was too young to manage anything when my parents disappeared although for them we never had a funeral, only a family gathering on the first anniversary of their disappearance.

Stella stayed on at Aunt Kate's and assisted with the arrangements. It was Aunt Kate's wish to be cremated; her ashes scattered into the Harbour, which she loved so dearly. Stella and I ensured that this final request was carried out, together we drove to Woollahra Point and walked to the edge of the water. Looking over the water we reminisced about all the fun times we had shared, the picnics we had taken in that exact location. Then finally, we scattered her ashes as she had requested.

"We will miss your hugs, we will miss your laughter, we will miss your spirit."

We strolled through the park back towards the car taking our time. My legs felt as though they had weights attached to them as my movement was hindered by the emotions, which engulfed my body. Stella was not saying much, I was sure she too, in her silence was reflecting over her life.

One week after we scattered Aunt Kate's ashes, I received a letter from a solicitor, inside was an invitation for the reading of Aunt Kate's Will. Stella also received the same letter and the both of us made the trip together. Stella and I sat motionless in the office as the formalities were explained. Then came the division of Aunt Kate's assets. I was bequeathed the house. Stella the car, Aunt Kate knew Stella loved her car. The money that she had in the bank was divided between the two of us. Stella would receive seventy five percent and I was to receive twenty five percent. As the solicitor read details I sat there amazed. I always knew that Aunt Kate was financially secure, although I never imagined her bank balance to be as high as the solicitor advised us it was. After the official reading had been concluded, the solicitor produced a letter, which Aunt Kate requested be read to the both of us.

Within the letter, Aunt Kate wrote of the affection she felt towards us both, how she had felt complete with us being in her life. Both of us struggled to fight off the tears, which were building in our eyes.

"You were the sunshine that brightened up my days, you

brought happiness within, when outside the world offered only despair. I trust you know how much you meant to me, how much pleasure and cheer you filled me with. I will always love you and so until we meet again you must be brave, you must be strong. Within the worlds garden you are daisies, if you are wondering why daisies, its because the flower stems over a lot of other flowers and its lovely and bright. In many ways, I think that relates to you. You stand so tall with confidence and you are colourful in every way, I will never forget you.

Love always and forever Kate"

Tears flowed uncontrollably down our cheeks and so after the solicitor concluded we left his office arm in arm. United once more by the sadness of the occasion, we returned to Aunt Kate's house where we made a toast in honour of Kate and the happiness she had brought into our lives.

CHAPTER SIXTEEN

Separatism, the state when one withdraws and detaches himself or herself from events which are happening around him or her, a state I was sinking into more and more as each day passed. I was forty years old, it was the time in my life when loving friends and family should have surrounded me. Yet, I was alone. Edward was still in Melbourne and Stella had moved back to her house at Coogee.

I wondered how many others in the world felt as lonely as I did. I wished that I could find someone I could sit with and talk to, someone I could confide in. I longed to be held by someone and yet when I was faced with a situation that may involve talking I would clam up. I would run away, I did not know what to say. I did not know if I was capable of loving another person. How could I love anyone else when I could not first find love within myself? I began to question the stability of Edward's and my relationship. I was, as they say, over the hill. On my birthday, I sat wondering how far down the hill I would have to slide before I would finally stop.

They say, money does not buy happiness and I can assure you it does not. I was financially secure, not only had I inherited my parents house, I had also inherited Aunt Kate's as well. Yet, I was not happy. Yes, I could afford all the luxuries of life, but believe me, luxuries are not worth anything if you don't have anyone around you to share them with, if you don't have anyone to sit and talk to.

As each day passed, I found myself drinking more and more. After Aunt Kate's death, I resigned from work. I couldn't face the world outside. Kate had described me as a daisy within the world's garden, all bright and colourful standing above all the rest. I didn't feel like a daisy and I certainly didn't feel bright and colourful.

I longed for Edward to return. I longed to be held within his arms. He would not be back for another eight months. I was not sure if I would last eight months. My days were passed in drinking until I could no longer keep track; days and nights all blurred together. The clock was no longer important; the number of drinks I had until I passed out determined time. The house was no longer immaculate. My depression was so severe that nothing else really mattered, it was as if everything else was thrown out the window.

Edward continued to telephone regularly. I told him of Aunt Kate's death and he felt helpless being in Melbourne. I assured him that I was fine, although I didn't tell him I had quit my job. Many times I would hear the telephone ring and couldn't be bothered to answer it. When Edward spoke to me, I would tell him I was suffering from the flu or simply tired if he questioned my vagueness. In our time of being together I had never heavily indulged in alcohol, therefore he had no reason to expect anything more. I explained the unanswered calls by saying I had been out visiting people, that my life was hectic. He believed me.

Christmas came around again, only three months until Edward would return to Sydney. I had been drinking heavily for about six months and felt the need to stop. I needed to pull my life together before he returned. Otherwise, he might not be impressed with what he found. At first, I thought giving up my drinking would be easy. However, it proved to be a difficult challenge. I had not realised how much I had depended on the alcohol, how much it had masked everything which was happening around me.

I strolled around the house, dust had settled on the furniture, bottles and food scraps where scattered over the kitchen benches. The fridge contained nothing edible, those contents, which remained inside looked like foreign objects, bottles and jars with mould around the tops held unrecognisable things inside. I couldn't believe my eyes, I couldn't believe I had let myself get into such a state. Alcohol is a powerful thing and I had let it control my life.

It took me, all of the next three months and a huge effort to get my act together; I employed the services of some decorators who came in and totally revamped the inside of the house. By the time all the renovations were complete, the interior looked nothing like it had when Aunt Kate was alive. The walls were now painted in orange and the wall-to-wall carpet was a deep purple. I was happy with my selection of colours. All the kitchen benches were replaced with orange laminex and the bathroom was also gutted, mosaic tiles were laid on the floor and I installed a new pink bath. These choices were all fashionable in those days. For the outside, I hired a gardener who lopped trees, cut hedges, repaired flowerbeds and kept up the general maintenance of the lawn. At the same time, I also decided it would be best to improve the outside appearance of my parents' house. The memories, which the house held prevented my return however, better and more regular maintenance and improved gardening would help maintain the property value should I decide to sell it at a later date. I was not overly concerned with the contents, all the furniture had been covered with large sheets and I felt this would suffice. By the time Edward returned to Sydney, he would not suspect anything had been wrong.

During this time, war had again reared its ugly head. Australia had been dragged into the Vietnam War and in 1964 the National Service was introduced. Numbered marbles drawn from a barrel determined who would be conscripted. This conscription applied to any man over twenty years of age whose date of birth was drawn. Edward was passed the age of being conscripted and I prayed he did not express any interest in joining the cause, I had missed him for nearly eighteen months. I was relieved he was older and wiser and did not know if I could bear the news of him having to fight in any war.

Conscription was like a hot potato; the freedom of choice was being stolen from many men, who were forced into the army against their will. If they failed to accept this instruction, they would be jailed for two years. Protesters marched the streets, blocking roads and battles broke out with police who tried to disperse the crowds.

All I wanted was to see Edward back in Sydney; his smiled burned deeply into my mind, as I waited to be in his arms where time was boundless. He had come to me like a vision, totally unexpected making me think I was part of a dream and I fell in love. Before he departed for Melbourne I told Edward he was the light shining in my once tired eyes, the passion I breathed, the soul I shared and the heart that beats in my chest full of desire. With Edward in my life, I was filled with butterflies that formed his name. It was as if we were made for each other, Edward was my needle in the haystack, a beautiful, wondrous find and I ached when we were apart.

Since his leaving, I had dropped down to the depths of despair, but then I had managed to climb my way out. I felt stronger than I had in years; I could handle anything that was placed before me, just as long as I was reunited with Edward.

I was lucky, Edward wanted no involvement in the war. Ray, one of Edward's colleagues in the Melbourne office, was not so lucky. Edward said Ray was devastated. He had been working with him for twelve months. Edward always described him as a quiet and gentle kind of guy. On hearing the news Edward said that Ray broke down into tears, comparing his actions to those of a little boy who had just discovered his pet dog had died. He had told Edward that he could not bear the thought of killing another human, that the sight of blood made him faint and he felt as though he had been trapped between a rock and a hard place. There was nothing Ray could do; it was either go to Vietnam or go to jail. Not liking either of his options, Ray made a radical decision, which shocked everyone; he took his own life. Another work colleague found him in his garage. He had connected a hose to the exhaust pipe of his Holden. Then, run the hose into the car window, put on some music and listened to it in the front seat of his car until the last breath left his body.

Edward was distressed by Ray's actions and appalled that any man could be drafted into the army against his will, to fight in another country's war. He was not a patriot, he believed in freedom of choice and the drafting took that freedom away. No matter how much he loved Australia and how proud he was to be an Australian he did not believe in fighting, what he believed was another country's war.

CHAPTER SEVENTEEN

Edward greeted me with open arms, when I opened the door. I had been expecting he would return to Sydney, the week after he arrived on my doorstep. We hugged each other as we had never hugged before, he was back. Edward was with me once more. Taking him by the hand, I dragged him inside. Our lips passionately met and we kissed until I felt as though I would fall down exhausted. Tears of happiness flowed from my eyes. I could not believe that after all that time he was again standing before me.

We sat and talked for hours, Edward explained that he had pleaded with his boss to return to Sydney so that he would not miss his mother's birthday. He had lied and stated his mother was turning seventy and that she would be devastated if her only son had missed such a special occasion. Pleased with his work, his boss agreed. Edward packed his belongings and took the next available flight to Sydney. From the airport, he got a cab straight to my house. I was surprised that he would use such tactics, he was a well-spoken and polite man with an honest face, and it never crossed my mind that he would be capable of such deception.

That night, we went to dinner at the same place we had gone on our first date. Both of us sat at the table with a grin from ear to ear.

Edward talked of his experiences in Melbourne; his employer had provided his accommodation. It was a one bedroom flat near St Kilda and he would catch the tram to work daily. On the weekend he would spend his time down by the water, there he would sit for hours and think of me back in Sydney. One weekend he ventured out of Melbourne and drove down the coast to Torquay, where he stayed overnight in a small hotel. He said all he could think about was returning to Sydney. When I told him of Aunt Kate's death, he became concerned, as I did not sound happy on the telephone. He was also concerned when he could not contact me, although he said he felt his worries ease when I assured him that I was fine and that I had been hectic with my social life. I sat there listening to him and felt bad that I could not have been honest with him. I wanted to tell him the truth, but when he told me that he had seriously considered throwing in his job and returning to my side, I knew I had done the correct thing by lying.

Edward loved his job and if my antics had forced him into resignation, he may have resented me later in life. Once he finished telling his tales I made up some stories and told him what I had been doing. He did know some of the things that had been happening, so I just fluffed them up a little by throwing in some parties and weekend trips away. I also advised him that I had resigned from my job, telling him that had only happened weeks before his return, due to my feeling of being unfulfilled. I did not tell him of the fortune I had in the bank due to the inheritance, rather I told him that I had managed to save some money and therefore I was intending to take some time out.

Edward knew that I had inherited my Aunt's house and so I invited him to live there with me. Before moving to Melbourne he had lived with his mother and had expressed an interest in moving out. I thought it would be ridiculous for him to search for new accommodation, when I was living in such a huge house. Before he could accept my invitation Edward said that he had some things he had to do, however, he would seriously consider my offer. He did have to see his mother, although, she was not celebrating a birthday in the near future. She too had missed her son and he had a duty to make sure she was all right.

Edward stayed the night, in the morning we sat down to breakfast and he said he would take his belongings to his mothers. I agreed and was sad to think he was leaving again. However, this time he was only travelling to Randwick, on the other side of Centennial Park and this thought eased my sadness. The distance between us would no longer restrict our seeing each other. Edward called to tell me he had arrived at his mothers and invited me over for dinner so we could finally be introduced. His mother was a nice lady, she told me how she had never seen her son so happy and how he never completed a conversation where I was not discussed. Prior to leaving after dinner Edward went to the bathroom, in his absence his mother took my hand and with a tear in her eye she said that she was happy Edward had met me. I could sense her words were sincere, I too was happy that I had met Edward and so I nodded my head and told her the same. She made me smile and I felt welcome in her house.

After two days of rest, Edward returned to work and in the next week, I did not see him that often. He was busy re-establishing his role within the Sydney operation. I was glad he had not thrown in the towel while in Melbourne. I was glad I did not tell him the truth about what I had been going through. On the Friday night, Edward telephoned to tell me he had received a promotion, his title was now chief financial officer. I was proud of him, his efforts had paid off and he asked if I would like to join him in a celebratory dinner, an invitation I promptly accepted.

Edward arrived at my house at exactly seven o'clock, he was always punctual and if he said seven o'clock you could be sure he would be there. In his hand, he held a single long stemmed red rose, which he handed to me when I opened the door. This time we did not go to our usual restaurant, although it was always very nice, this time Edward had made reservations at a very classy restaurant in North Sydney.

A gentleman in a tuxedo greeted us at the door and asked if he could take out coats. I had never been into a restaurant of such class, soft music played in the background and candles flickered on every table. The main meal was superb, never in my life had I tasted roasted lamb that just melted in my mouth. All the vegetables were cooked to perfection and the wine we drank was soft and flavoursome with a spicy fruit flavour and a lingering finish.

I did not believe the evening could get any better. Edward took my hand across the table and he gently rubbed the back of it, as he spoke of his past and the future he dreamed of, which would include me. Although, the restaurant had many patrons, tables were set wide enough apart so that a feeling of privacy was maintained. A waiter, who came to the table wanting to know if we were interested in desserts, interrupted our discussions. Initially, I declined the offer, although Edward took the menu and said he would make a selection on my behalf. I agreed, how could I disagree with the man of my dreams, he had swept me off my feet, taken me to an expensive restaurant and filled my night with flattery.

Edward made a selection and the waiter disappeared, moments later he returned carrying a large bowl of strawberries that had a scoop of ice cream sitting on top. It was what I saw on top of the ice cream that caught my eye. Tears filled my eyes as Edward removed the ring from the ice cream with a spoon, placed it into his mouth, gently took my left hand while dropping to one knee. Then with the ring between his lips, he slipped it onto my finger.

"Will you marry me, will you make me the happiest man alive?"

I was speechless; you could have knocked me over with a feather and without any hesitation I said, "Yes."

We never ate the strawberries; both of us were too overcome by emotion. Previously, I had only ever dreamt of such romantic events and now they were actually real. Restaurant patrons clapped; complete strangers congratulated our announcement. I would soon be Mrs. Rutherford.

Leaving the restaurant, I found it difficult to contain my happiness. Holding hands, we walked down the street, eventually finding a cab that dropped us back to my home in Paddington. Edward stayed the night.

The next day we visited his mother, Edward told her that I had accepted his proposal and I showed off my ring, before we collected Edward's belongings. Edward moved in and wedding preparations were under-way. Both of us agreed, we would have only a small wedding. I did not have many I wanted to invite. The invitation list consisted of my aunt and uncle, Stella, Edward's family and some of his work friends. In all, there were a dozen of us, not too many, not too few. Just those who we cared about and considered close.

Our Wedding date would be set for Saturday, 11th September that same year. I was happy with this date. I knew that age had no bearing on what an individual could or could not do but psychologically I felt better knowing that I would scrape into marriage while still forty, even if it was only by a few days.

I ordered the flowers, Mrs. Rutherford, Edward's mother insisted she would make the cake, Edward organised cars and both of us chose the church and restaurant for our reception. It was all coming together; my life was coming together.

CHAPTER EIGHTEEN

On the eve of June twenty-nine 1965, I broke down; it was one year since Aunt Kate had died. The plans for my wedding were well under way and the wedding date had been set for September Eleven. Although I frequently thought of Aunt Kate, over the past few months I had been busy organising things and had lost track of time. All my focus had been on counting down the days to my wedding, with no time for other issues.

Stella telephoned that night; there was sadness in her voice. It was only then, I realised the significance of the day. I had not thought of Aunt Kate at all for the entire day. I could not believe that I could dismiss such an important date. I sat at the kitchen table, spread out before me was paperwork relating to the organisation of my wedding. I was lost for words, I pulled my feet up on to the chair I sat on and lowered my chin to my right knee. Cuddling my knees with my left arm, I held the telephone in my right hand and asked if Stella was all right. She replied that she would be fine. She was just upset as she missed Kate and did not know how she would ever find anyone else like her.

"No matter how rare true love is, true friendship is even rarer and above all else I always considered her a true friend. She was an inspirational person, it was an honour and a privilege knowing her, I only wish she was still here so I could tell her." She was crying as she spoke and I knew she was not fine. I too was crying, the tears that had welled in my eyes now rolled down my cheeks.

I had to leave my wedding preparations; I had to be with Stella. I told her I would come to her and asked if she was at home, she replied that she was and I told her to stay there, I would soon be over. Hanging up the telephone I grabbed for some paper and wrote Edward a note, telling him I had to go over to Stella, that she was in need of a friend and that I would return when I was able to.

I made it to Stella's in about fifteen minutes; the front door was open, so I walked straight in. At first, I feared she may have left and gone for a walk to the beach. Hurriedly, I scanned the lounge then the kitchen, passing the bathroom I also checked that she was not there. Then I heard sobbing, it was coming from her bedroom, inside I found her laying on her bed, she had been drinking, I could smell the alcohol in the air. Without any further delay, I climbed on her bed and placed my arms around her. There I sat still and without saying a word I caressed her hair, pulling back those strands that covered her mournful face. I could do nothing to take away the pain she was feeling, I could only try to give her solace as I embraced her on her bed. I could feel her heart beating rapidly as the sounds of her sobbing filled the room. Together we lay on the bed, again we were united in a time of sadness.

After a few quite moments, Stella started to talk; she was telling me about the first time she met Kate. I had never asked how they had met; I only understood the strong feelings they had towards each other. Her voice was soft and shaky as she spoke. To my amazement, both had met at the scene of an accident. A young child had been hit by a car while riding his bicycle. Both had witnessed the accident and had hurried over to offer assistance. Stella paused; a smile came to her face. Then she continued.

"Making our way to the boy we both lowered our heads at the same time and hit foreheads. Once we established things at the scene were all right and the injuries sustained were minor, we decided to visit the pub, which was on the adjacent corner for a quick drink. It was over this drink we realised we were very much alike and so we continued to stay in touch."

Never would I have imagined that two people could have met under such strange circumstances. I had always presumed that they had met at a dinner or social function involving the arts. Maybe even while completing their studies at University, but not at the scene of an accident that was way too bizarre, also considering they had bumped heads just as Edward and I had.

For hours, we lay on the bed reminiscing over the fun times we all shared together. The long walks we would take down along the beaches with a picnic basket, blanket and a kite, which we would watch, soar in the sky for hours at a time. The water fights we would have during hot summer days, the camping adventures and day trips to the mountains. There were far too many happy times to mention. Never did I hear a cross word spoken; never did I hear either raise their voices. I was glad my Aunt Kate had met Stella, I was glad Stella had met Aunt Kate. The closeness they shared was rare. Although, I was very much upset about losing Aunt Kate, I knew my sadness could never equal that felt by Stella. I also knew, both were very fortunate to have shared their lives.

After lying on the bed we decided we should have a drink, with all the talking both of us had worked up a thirst and so we ventured into the lounge room where Stella poured us both a scotch. Handing me my glass she proceeded over to the stereo where she picked out an Ella

Fitzgerald record turned up the volume and played it from start to finish. For that time our discussions ceased, instead we both sang and shared the occasional dance. Fate had taken Aunt Kate from us, but nothing could steal away the memories we held so close to our hearts. As I closed my eyes, I imagined Aunt Kate was with us, typically she would either have been up dancing with us or back at the bar asking if there were any other drink orders. Laughter, a feeling of great happiness and love would have filled the air.

Once the record completed, Stella let out a loud sigh and asked me if I would stay the night with her. She had calmed down a lot, but a few kind words, dancing, singing and drinks were not enough to take away the loneliness and sadness she felt. Agreeing to her request, feeling slightly intoxicated and very tired I suggested we head off to bed. Stella was like a big sister to me, for years she had watched over me and offered advice whenever I was in need. Staying the night with her was the very least I could do. I only wished I could do more for her. I only wished I knew how I could help take her pain away. Climbing into bed, I placed my arms around her and within seconds, I was asleep.

Waking in the morning, I looked over to see Stella fast asleep. My arm was still over her, so I gently removed it, climbed out of bed and proceeded into the kitchen where I decided I would make her breakfast. It had been years since I had prepared anything for anyone and so looking through her cupboards and fridge I became nervous. Turning the kettle on, I decided coffee and toast would suffice.

By the time the kettle boiled, I heard Stella moving around in the bathroom and so I yelled to her and told her that coffee and toast were ready. Together we ate breakfast and thanked each other for the night; both of us had benefited by spending time together.

Soon after eating, we parted company, Stella had an appointment in the city at lunchtime and I had to get back to my wedding arrangements. On our parting hug, I assured her that she would be all right and reminded her that I would always be there for her, no matter what time of the day or night. I was a telephone call away and that was something I wanted her to be sure of.

CHAPTER NINETEEN

There was no shortage of morning glory on the Eleventh of September 1965; I was getting married to the man of my dreams. After struggling from within my depths of despair, my life was beginning to turn around; there was a light at the end of the tunnel. To my amazement, I was getting married and had just scraped in still being forty years old. For so long, I had believed that I was destined never to find happiness, never to marry, believing I would live my life a lonely spinster.

Stella arrived at my house in the early hours of the morning; she was excited and nervous. I had asked her to walk me down the aisle and to give me away. I knew it was not the conventional thing to do, but I had no father or man that was able to fill such a role. Stella had accepted my request, stating that it would be an honour. My stomach was doing somersaults, I needed a drink, and I needed something to calm my nerves. Stella went to the kitchen and poured us both a scotch, it was only just after nine o'clock and the wedding was still over three hours away, the scotch would do us well.

As Stella filed and painted my nails in a soft pink nail polish I wondered what Edward was doing, I wondered if he felt as nervous as I did. I felt incredibly lucky, all the hard times I had experienced were behind me, the obstacles, which had once stood before me had given me strength. *All good things come to those who wait,* I thought. This was my time, my day and no one would stand in my way, no one had stopped me from doing anything before and no one would now. I thought of my parents, Bugsy, my grandma and Aunt Kate, I wondered what they would say if they could see me now.

Stella finished my nails and sat back in the lounge, she had a puzzled look on her face.

"What are you thinking Shirley?" she asked. To which I replied "Nothing, I was just going through all the preparations to ensure everything was how it should be." She smiled and lent forward hugging me, "Everything will be fine, you'll see, all good things come to those who wait." How ironic, I thought, that she would say those words, especially since I had just been thinking the exact thing moments before. I hugged her and whispered in her ear that Aunt Kate was watching us, so we had better be on our best behaviour. She giggled, kissed me on the cheek and pulled away, giving me a wink she sat on the lounge with a grin from ear to ear.

I understood why Aunt Kate and Stella had been so close and I appreciated Stella being with me, on my special day. She had a wonderful smile, that was contagious and eyes that could look right into me, without making me feel nervous. I had passed the stage in my life where I had challenged myself to show no emotion, I too sat on the lounge with a grin from ear to ear.

With plenty of time remaining, before we would be picked up for the church both Stella and I agreed another scotch would do no harm. There were only three things, which I was required to do before being picked up, put on my dress, do my hair and my make-up. The scotch would ease our nerves and put us in the mood for some serious celebrating.

Stella went to the kitchen and made us a fresh scotch, this time stronger than the last; I took a gulp and sat on the lounge looking around the room. There had been so many parties held in this room, if the walls could talk, they would tell so many tales.

My stomach began doing somersaults again, I took Stella by the hand and told her that I loved her and cherished her friendship. I had regretted not saying those words to my aunt Kate. Although, I hoped she knew what she had meant to me, I could not be sure and I was not going to let this moment pass without telling Stella. Tears welled in her eyes as she clasped my hand.

"You are one of the most important people in my life and I love you too Shirley Rumming, for in this world of ours to others you may just be another person, but to me you are the world."

We both took another swig of our scotch and then I yanked Stella's hand pulling her off the lounge and up the stairs to my bedroom. Inside the door hung my wedding dress, it was beautiful, white silk with a sheer lace and a bow at the back. It had taken me months to find. Stella was not only giving me away but also filling the role of my bridesmaid. Her dress hung in Aunt Kate's old room; we had picked the dresses together. Hers was burgundy, the top of the dress was lace with a nearly straight drop from the waistline, and she looked stunning in it. Both of us got changed and hurried to the mirror where we stood admiring each other, laughing for a moment like two schoolgirls. It was time to do my make-up and so I sat on the chair in front of my dresser, applying everything as I had rehearsed. Stella stood beside me, giving me advice during the application, then we were ready for our hairstyling. I did not want anything too outrageous or puffy. I did not go much for the bee hive style, which was all the rage so Stella offered to braid it back away from my face. Within a few minutes, we had transformed ourselves and I was now ready to be married.

The car turned up just as we made it back down to the lounge. Stella called out to the driver and told him we would be a few minutes. I inhaled deeply and sighed loudly. We both made one final check to ensure everything was as it should be, then Stella took me by the arm and we walked out the front door down to the gate. The next time I would step foot in this house I would be Mrs. Rutherford. I felt as though I was a princess in a fairytale. I looked at my watch and noticed we were late. Stella assured me that everything would be wonderful and that brides were supposed to be late, that was tradition.

Edward was pacing back and forth on the steps of the church as we turned the corner. No doubt, he was as nervous as I was. Spotting our car he grabbed the arm of Vaughan LeStrange his best man, Vaughan worked as the caretaker of a property out near Orange and from what Edward told me he was an honest and kind person. The two had maintained a friendship since meeting in kindergarten. Although, their lives took on very different paths, they knew they could count on each other and when they caught up, it was as if time had stood still and they would start up where they had left off. Dashing into the church, the few guests who stood in their company followed. Climbing out of the car I heard the organ playing, my nose became tingly as tears filled my eyes. Stella told me to pull myself together and I did, then we made our way to the church doors. It was darker inside and it took me a moment for my eyes to adjust. Edward stood near the altar, he was a handsome sight, I could tell he was nervous, he was twitching his hands and swaying from side to side.

Before I knew it we were down the aisle and Edward was standing before me, his beautiful eyes looking at me, his captivating lips waiting to be kissed. I don't recall very much of the service, I think it is because I was so overwhelmed by my emotions. As Edward stood before me, all I wanted to do was to make him mine, there was no way I was going to let him go. I do remember the important parts of the service; the "I do", the exchanging of our rings and last but not least, the moment when we finally sealed our marriage with a kiss. Edward was finally mine.

Confetti was thrown all over us, as we left the church making our way to The Royal Botanic Gardens for photos. Then we headed back to the reception, where our family and close friends met us with a toast to our everlasting happiness. We ate, drank, danced, and heard telegrams offering congratulations then finally just before midnight we departed to our honeymoon suite in the Hilton Hotel. The wedding was perfect, just as we had wanted and planned.

With Edward's busy work commitments we could not take a vacation, so instead we opted to have one night alone which would be followed by a well-planned honeymoon in the future.

Approaching our room Edward took me by the arm and swept me off my feet, then he opened the door and carried me to the bed. It was a night full of passion like I had never experienced before, our bodies twisted and turned around each other. Edward was like a ravenous animal and I was only too happy to please his every desire.

By the time the sun rose in the morning, the bed had been demolished. Clothes and blankets were strewn across the room. Edward lay naked on the bed next to me, exhausted from our night of lovemaking. I placed my hand gently on his stomach and slowly moved it upwards to his chest where I rested it there, slowly caressing his left nipple. Edward opened his eyes and looked over to me, he smiled and lent over kissing me.

"Good Morning Mrs. Rutherford."

I kissed him again and as we embraced his tongue danced with mine. Within moments, we were again enjoying extreme delight, as we had the night before. Pure ecstasy engulfed my body as Edward thrust his body against mine and again we made love.It was the most orgasmic experience I had ever had and as it turned out the most orgasmic experience, I would ever have.

Ten weeks after we had first consummated our marriage my world was sent into a spin, I was pregnant. Shock engulfed my body; I was forty one years old and pregnant. Staring at the doctor in disbelief, I desperately tried to acknowledge what he was saying. Surely I was passed the age of being able to conceive a child, for god sake, women were having babies in their twenties and thirties, maybe even prior to being twenty, but not over forty. Edward and I had discussed having children, both of us said we would love to have a child of our own. We acknowledged our age could play a major factor in this becoming a reality. For us, a child was not a necessity and therefore we agreed we should let nature take its course. However, we never really imagined that I would fall pregnant so easily and so quickly.

"How can this be?" I stammered.

"Oh it is very possible to have a child at your age, of course it is not a common occurrence, but it is possible," the doctor nodded.

As the news sunk in, I began to wonder how Edward would react.

Cupping my tummy, I listened to the doctor as he explained all the risks involved with my pregnancy. Blood pressure, birth defects, ectopic pregnancy or even miscarriage, the list went on and on and every issue raised was a real concern. However, he assured me with close monitoring it was not impossible to have a healthy baby, after all I had overcome the biggest obstacle of all, which was falling pregnant in the first place.

Sitting Edward down that evening his jaw dropped as I broke the news.

"Wow!" he said, stunned.

"We are going to be parents," looking at him I searched for a reaction.

After what seemed an eternity, Edward leaped from his chair and threw his arms around me.

"Oh my God I am going to be a daddy, we are going to be parents."

Excitement filled the air; Edward was over the moon. Nothing could be better, I was in love with a man who adored me and together we were going to have a baby. Edward said I had the glow of a pregnant woman and he would fuss over my every move. Everyday he would telephone from work to make sure I was feeling well and in the evening he made every attempt to make it home at a reasonable time.

Silently, I worried about being pregnant at such a late age. There was no way that I could ignore the statistics, being an older mum to be, was not going to be easy.

Yet, with every worrying thought, I reminded myself of my doctor's words, *it is very possible to have a child at your age.*

Each morning I would stand naked in front of the mirror and study myself. Gently running my hands over my tummy, I would quietly say my own positive affirmation, " I am healthy, my baby is healthy, I am blessed, we are blessed."

And to my surprise, everyone expressed great delight at our news.

Christmas was upon us before we knew it and gone just as fast. Christmas day was spent with Edward's family. He had a nice family; they were honest to each other and did not backstab one another like I had seen in many families. For lunch we feasted on ham, pork, turkey and roasted vegetables. This was followed by pudding with sixpence and shillings. His mother was renowned for her Christmas puddings and after taking one bite I could tell why. After Christmas lunch we called in to visit Stella, she had some friends over for her celebrations and so we joined them for drinks. I was pleased that Edward liked Stella. She had been in my life for over twenty years and was very important to me. After drinks we said our farewells and took a stroll along Gordon Bay. I was in need of a walk as I had eaten so much that I felt I would explode. Walking along the waters edge I was surprised at how many families were there, how many couples sat on picnic blankets. I had never been to the beach on a Christmas day and therefore I naturally believed everyone spent the day at home or at the house of a friend or relative.

Firecracker's lit the skies around us, as people in the streets began the countdown for the New Year, 1965 was over. Edward and I kissed and made a toast to the New Year, to the first full year that we would enjoy being husband and wife. The year we would become a family, for our little bundle of joy was growing well and would soon be with us. Life, could not get any better, life was perfect.

Edward returned to work in the second week of January, he was so happy in his job. His efforts had been rewarded and he was determined to be a success. I continued to stay at home and began to put on weight really fast. By the time I was seven months I had packed on so much weight, it became uncomfortable to do much more than lie down and that too, was uncomfortable at times.

Edward would join me at the doctor's surgery for regular check ups, the doctor was concerned about my blood pressure and this made Edward stress. Continually, I assured him that everything would be fine. I had always wanted to have a natural birth; however, the doctor advised me that I might have to have a caesarean due to my blood pressure and also to the size and position of the baby.

Silently, I worried about my baby, I knew my blood pressure was high and throughout the pregnancy, I had not been able to escape morning sickness. Every so often, I would feel severe pains in my stomach and not having had a baby before I advised the doctor. He assured me that I should expect some pain due to my size, however, he also said that should they become more severe then I should take myself to the hospital.

For weeks, I continued pottering around the house and venturing into Sydney to shop, although I did not want to over-exert myself, I wanted to maintain some level of fitness. The pains continued to be felt to the same degree and I continued to assure myself that everything would be fine. From the doctor's tests and the feeling of my baby's kicking everything would turn out as we wished and within the next two months Edward and I would have our first child.

On May twenty third, I collapsed down stairs in the lounge room, Edward was at work. My pain had returned, this time it was worst than ever, I struggled to get to the telephone and called for an ambulance. Something was wrong, something was definitely wrong. Lying on the floor I could no longer feel my baby move. Tears streamed from my eyes as I screamed, "No, not my baby, don't take my baby!"

The ambulance turned up within minutes, by that stage I was hysterical. My face was a picture of anguish and distress. Quickly they placed an oxygen mask over my face and lifted me onto the stretcher. As they wheeled me to the ambulance, I yelled at the officer that I needed to contact Edward. He assured me that everything would be all right and they would contact Edward as soon as possible.

The siren blared as we sped to the hospital; both ambulance officers continually assured me that everything would be fine. One of them checked my blood pressure and heart. My baby still had not kicked again, I knew things would not be all right. Something was definitely wrong and I feared at that moment I had lost my baby.

Another team of medical personnel was waiting for us at the hospital and immediately I was rushed down the hallway. A doctor walked beside the stretcher advising me, if there was to be any chance they could save my baby, he would have had to do an emergency caesarean. I signed the consent forms and into surgery I went, praying for my baby like I had never prayed before.

CHAPTER TWENTY

Like a dead woman walking, dazed and confused I strolled around the hospital; earlier the doctors had been forced to sedate me due to my hysterics. But now, I had woken, I was in pain, despondent and consumed by guilt, my baby was gone. Nothing could have prepared me for this immeasurable heartache. I had lost my baby. Both Edward and I were devastated, our baby son was gone. I was pining for that last hug, that last special moment, in which I could hold my little man, just one last moment, a moment that was not meant to be. We only got to see him briefly before the nurses took him away. His hands were so tiny and he had a full head of hair, jet-black just like Edward's, he was beautiful and looked just like an angel, so still and at peace. I held him tightly to my chest and could not stop my uncontrollable crying, Edward sat next to me and together we named our little boy, Jake. Life could be cruel, life was not meant to be like this.

Had I left it too late in life to conceive a child? Had this loss been a punishment, for the wrongdoing I had committed in my younger years? Was I, just the type of person who was never destined to find real happiness?

I returned to my hospital bed and I refused to venture outside for days. My doctor recommended I see a therapist who could help me come to terms with what had happened. All the "what if" scenarios whizzed around in my head. What if I had rested more during my pregnancy? What if I had eaten better foods? Was it something I did, that made my baby die?

The doctor assured me, that I was not to blame. The umbilical cord had twisted around my baby's throat. There was nothing anyone could have done to prevent this. There had been no way of knowing it would happen.

Stella soon heard the news of my loss and came to my side to comfort me. What I found hardest, was answering questions people asked. Many people stayed away, not wanting to visit. I understand now that for many it is easy to say nothing rather than to say something, which may not sound as they intended. Sad occasions are always hard for everyone; grief can be very overwhelming especially when it involves the loss of a baby.

The funeral for little Jake was the hardest thing I had to endure in my life. Edward walked beside me supporting most of my weight. My legs felt as though they were jelly, my heart as though it had been torn in two. The air was hot and humid, between sobs I struggled to inhale. My blouse was wet, wet with perspiration and tears, my make-up had run; my eyes were like those of a Panda bear.

Stella came and sat beside me, she was always a comfort. Tears welled up behind my sunglasses so much so that my vision became blurred. Edward released the hold he had on my hand and walked to the podium. Bravely he spoke of Jake, who had been with us for such a short time but who had touched us so deeply and changed our lives forever. It was time for us to say our goodbyes, and while I could acknowledge the finality of a funeral, I knew my heart would carry the scars forever.

The wake was held back at our house and was an exceptionally hard experience, unlike a wake for an adult there were no tales to be told. No misadventures to be laughed about, no embarrassing situations to be remembered, only the loss of our son who did not get a chance at life. Edward stood next to me, although even with his closeness, I sensed a distance between us. After the wake, I was left with emptiness. Another chapter in my life had closed, what the next one held in store for me I could only imagine. I could only hope it was better than the last. Edward insisted we leave the tidying up until the morning. He looked into my eyes and said I needed to rest, we both needed to rest and he took me by the hand up to our bedroom.

Once in bed, I lay there staring at the ceiling. I was not sure if Edward's idea of an early night was as good as he had intended. My mind was racing at a million miles an hour. I recalled the funeral of Bugsy, it too had been a sad occasion but at least for Bugsy I had been able to recall the smile I had witnessed on his face. He had experienced joy, love and laughter, Jake was stolen from us. How could any God steal an innocent baby? My grief soon changed to anger, as I lay on the bed with my jaw clenched tight, I could feel my nostrils flaring, my eyes glaring at the ceiling. I was searching for an answer, listening to hear if a voice would explain to me, why I had lost baby Jake.

Rolling over, I faced Edward. He was sound asleep. We had both been through an exhausting ordeal and Edward could fall asleep at the drop of a hat. Lying there next to me, he looked so peaceful as if he had no care in the world, I wondered what he was thinking, every so often, his eyes would flicker and his body would twitch. Gently I rose from the bed and went to the bathroom, I still had some sedatives the doctor had prescribed for me and this was definitely a time I needed something to go to sleep. Opening the jar, I took out one and for a moment contemplated taking a handful, putting an end to the misery seemed an easy way out. From the bedroom, I heard Edward moving restlessly in the bed, I dropped the tablets back in the jar, only keeping out the one, took a glass of water and swallowed it.

By the time I made it back to bed Edward was stretched out diagonally, gently I shoved him over to his side and climbed in. Within minutes, I was asleep, the tablets were potent and after swallowing just one I had little time to ponder. Waking in the morning I found myself in an empty bed, Edward was nowhere in sight, downstairs was silent. For a moment I thought he might have taken a stroll out to the pond in the backyard, however, looking from the bedroom window I could not see him anywhere.

It was just after ten in the morning and my next thought was that Edward might have taken a walk to clear his thoughts or maybe grab the newspaper. Slowly I pulled myself together and made my way down to the kitchen, there I prepared myself a cup of tea and sat on the stool looking out the window. Outside I could already see a heat haze rising from the pavement, it was unusually warm for that time of the year and I was sure we would again see the mercury rise, as we had yesterday.

By the time eleven o'clock came around there was still no sign of Edward. This concerned me. Frantically, I began to search for a note that he may have left. Finally, after searching the kitchen and the lounge room I returned upstairs to our bedroom. On my bedside table, I found a note. Relieved, I sat on the bed and read it. Edward had decided to go into work for the morning, he assured me that he would be home for lunch, he also wrote that he did not want to disturb me so he had left me to sleep. I was upset that he had gone to work, however, happy that there had not been a problem, obviously people have different mechanisms, which are activated as a way of dealing with different situations. Edward's was to focus on his work and I had to respect this.

Lunchtime arrived and in walked Edward, he was home as promised, under his arm, he carried a pile of paperwork. It was obvious he intended to stay at home with me and so he would not fall behind with his busy work schedule he had decided to bring some work home.

Edward worked from home a lot over the next three weeks, by the time he decided to go back into the office full time I was relieved. I loved him, but he was starting to send me crazy, his fussing was enough to send anyone up the wall. Edward's executive position required him to be very meticulous and pedantic, these were two qualities Edward had brought home with him, two qualities I would have preferred he left at work.

Over time, my emotional reactions manifested into something much greater than feelings of everyday unhappiness or sadness. My feelings were more intense than those of unhappiness felt in daily life. I became anxious and was being hit by waves of panic attacks, which consumed my body leaving me with a feeling, that the world was closing in around me. I could not breathe; it was as if a fist was being rammed up my throat from the depths of my churning stomach, choking my air supply. My sleep patterns became disturbed, nightmares from the past returned and whilst my appetite decreased my fear increased. My world was collapsing. I had to act; I needed medical assistance, the feeling of overwhelming sadness was not only affecting my life but also devouring it.

Diagnosed with depression, I was prescribed with anti-depressant medication, which I was told would take one to four weeks to achieve positive effects. I had every reason to be depressed and I was sick and tired of Edward dictating what he felt I needed and what I should be doing. *"You need to get up and go out…You need to be surrounded by friends and family…You need to talk."* I questioned if he thought I was an idiot, incapable of recognising my needs, unable to decide what I should or shouldn't do. I knew what I needed, I lived in my body, I heard my thoughts, and I felt my feelings. I needed time to heal. All I felt like doing was screaming at him, telling him to get off my back. All I felt like doing was withdrawing. I needed alone time, time to sob, time to grieve, time to digest everything.

Some days, my motivation level was that low I would remain in bed, only rising when I expected Edward would soon be home. I was in search of so many answers and I did not want to be answering or justifying my actions to anyone. How could anyone who had never suffered from depression be able to dictate advice on a subject they had no first hand knowledge of? How easy it is for an outsider to say *"Get over it…You will be right… Life goes on."* It's like saying a witness to a plane crash has the right to tell a survivor of the crash how to cope. If they themselves hadn't experienced the plane crash first hand then how would they truly know, they are an outsider, merely an onlooker.

In life, we are told that we should embrace every moment, for without the bad it makes it more difficult to appreciate the good. The struggles in life are what make us strong; the challenges in life are what we conquer. No matter how big or small they all have relevance. However, no one sets us up for the unexpected challenges we are sometimes required to face. I had never been exposed to anyone who had experienced the loss of a child. I knew of no one who had experienced such a devastating tragedy. How could anyone embrace tragedy?

It was going to take time and it did take time. No one telling me anything different changed my grieving process and recovery. Wondering or questioning how long the depression would last only added additional pressure. My mind was like a jigsaw puzzle, all its pieces scattered within the confines of my head. How long it was going to take for the all the pieces to come together, could not be known.

Gradually, the medication took effect and I came to terms with my loss. Little by little, I started to recognise moments, events and objects that made me smile. I could not change what had happened. I would never forget what happened. The only thing I could do was accept it. Not casting any judgement, merely accepting it, focusing on the present moment, being mindful of my surroundings and those within it without dwelling on the past or fearing the future, my life became brighter. I began to appreciate the smaller niceties, a walk outside in the warmth of the sun, the feeling of being submerged in a warm bubble bath. The surprise of Edward walking through the front door holding a bunch of flowers, all these things had to be regarded as special. Edward loved me and I loved him with all my heart and more. I was awakened to mindfulness, the ability to pay attention in a particular way on purpose in the present moment and non-judgementally. I was alive in the present moment, therefore my energies would only be wasted if focused on a time other than where they were actually required, in the here and now.

CHAPTER TWENTY-ONE

The news of my pregnancy brought joy and extreme worry. I could not bear to lose another baby and I had been apprehensive at the thought of falling pregnant again. Yet, Edward had convinced me, we must continue with our lives, he had said if a person falls down, they don't just stay where they fall for the rest of their lives they get up and continue on. I understood where he was coming from but my grief was still so raw. What if becoming pregnant was just history repeating itself? This pregnancy could be my worst nightmare. It was not Edward who would have a new life form and grow within him. He did not feel our baby's movement. He never suffered from morning sickness nor did he experience the same attachment as I did, the closeness of a mothers bond.

I knew Edward dreamed of a family. The loss of our son had hit him hard. While I expressed my devastation in waves of hysterics, followed by a long period of depression, Edward had retreated within himself; his words were very few, as he immersed himself in his work. We took every precaution possible. I watched my diet and began a program of light exercise, in which I would take a daily stroll around the back garden. Edward insisted on making regular visits to the doctor again, however this time I was sure he would have been happy to see me placed in hospital where I could receive constant observations. I was worried I may suffer a miscarriage. While Edward was paranoid, we would experience another loss.

The nursery, which we had started to decorate when I was pregnant with Jake, remained untouched. I could see no use in completing decorations, when I was not confident about my outcome. I would walk into the nursery when Edward was not at home and sit for hours. Gently, I would rub my stomach and talk to my baby. I would play soft music to it and pick up some of the soft toys we had bought introducing them to our baby. I had heard this was good therapy. That it helped the baby relax and although I was not sure if it would have any bearing on the outcome, I thought it was worth a try. Anything was worth a try, if there was the slightest chance it would help with the successful birth of our child.

Stella came to visit me on a regular basis, just as she had throughout my last pregnancy; she realised that I was in a fragile state, maybe even more so than Edward did. She had no children of her own and together we would sit in the nursery, she would make silly voices impersonating the soft toys. Kneeling down beside me, she introduced herself to our baby and gently massaged my stomach. Every visit she would kiss my stomach and remind our baby who she was and how she would be there should our baby ever need anything. She was acting just as Aunt Kate would have, had she still been with us and I cherished every moment we shared. She was so thoughtful and caring, I did not need to ask for her visits, it was as if she knew when I required cheering up.

At seven months into my pregnancy, I visited the doctor; he was again worried about my blood pressure although, he was happier with my overall fitness. My morning sickness disappeared after the first few months and this time I did not suffer with the severe pains I had experienced last time. I was confident everything would be all right, although I could not help but to worry, I was definitely more confident than I had been before.

Two weeks before I was due to give birth, I began to feel pain in my stomach, my baby was moving inside me, but the pains which had haunted me throughout my last pregnancy had returned. I telephoned Edward at the office and hearing the concern in my voice he too became concerned and advised me to lie down, as he would be home soon. Within half an hour, Edward was at home and he carefully assisted me to the car before driving to the hospital. Leaving me in the emergency parking bay, he raced through the doors and yelled for a doctor.

Within a matter of seconds, a doctor burst back out through the door, with an assistant wheeling a wheel chair. Gently they assisted me into the wheel chair and wheeled me inside to an examination room. The doctor checked me right over, he listened to our baby and assured me it was not stressed, but suggested I remain in hospital until my baby was born. In the hospital, they would keep me under close observation and if the pain increased, they would perform another caesarean.

Edward came into the room once the doctor completed my examination; beads of sweat covered his forehead. I could see he feared it would be a repeat performance of Jake. Calming him down took some time, I gently rubbed his hand over my stomach letting him feel our baby's kicks, assuring him I was in the best possible place and we would soon have ourselves a happy healthy baby.

The doctor returned to the examination room and advised he had found me a bed in ward seven. Edward waited with me until they took me to my new room. Then, he left to go and collect some clothes and toiletries that I would need for my stay. He also said that he would telephone Stella and his mother so they would not be alarmed should they go to the house and find nobody home.

When Edward returned Stella was with him, she said that she had sensed something was wrong, so had gone to the house. Finding no one there frightened her and she said she was relieved when in minutes Edward drove into the driveway. In her arms, she carried a bright and colourful bunch of flowers, which she had purchased from the florist near the front entry of the hospital.

"For my special girl and my little baby friend," she said as she placed them in the vase, which sat on my bedside table. She then lent over and hugged me whispering in my ear that she would go and fetch some water so I could be alone with Edward.

I could see that he was uneasy sitting on the bed beside me and asked him if he was all right. As it turned out, he had an urgent meeting scheduled at work for that afternoon, it was a large business deal that he should not miss. I assured him that I would be fine and by the time Stella returned to the room, Edward had left. Before leaving he guaranteed he would return later that night, during visiting hours and kissed me on the cheek.

Stella scanned the room when she returned with the vase full of flowers and water. She was puzzled as to where Edward had gone. I explained to her that he had to attend an important business meeting and by the look on her face, I could tell she was annoyed with Edward's prioritising. Stella stayed with me for the rest of the afternoon; she gently massaged my stomach and feet while talking to my baby in the strange voices I had heard so many times before. Together we laughed and joked and by the time she left when my dinner was delivered my worries had all but disappeared.

The evening visiting hours came and went but there was no sign of Edward. It was obvious, that his business meeting had taken longer than expected and so I rolled over, closed my eyes and went to sleep. Throughout the night, I woke from bells and thuds heard out in the hallway, the hallway was well lit and so I rolled over onto my right side and placed a pillow over my head. By the time the sun rose, I felt I had only been asleep for a few minutes. Breakfast was delivered at seven, I was not very hungry and the food did not look at all appealing so I just ate my toast with a thin spread of marmalade jam. The toast was cold and I washed it down with a cold and very weak cup of tea.

When I finished breakfast, a nurse entered my room and asked if I would like to take a shower to freshen up. The shower sounded like a wonderful idea and as it turned out it was the hottest thing I had experienced that morning. Returning to my bed feeling refreshed I found that it had been made and my pillows had been fluffed and so I walked to the window drew the blinds closed, climbed back into bed and went back to sleep.

Before I knew it, I was woken for lunch; roast beef and tomato sandwiches accompanied by a container of two fruits, which looked a lot more appetising than breakfast had. I devoured it all within a matter of minutes then asked the nurse if I could take a stroll out to the garden to get some fresh air. She agreed the fresh air would do me well, but said that she would fetch a wheelchair as she did not want to see me over exerting myself and so together we went to the garden. We returned to my room a short time later, where I climbed back into bed and relaxed until dinnertime. Edward turned up at the nightly visiting hours, apologised profusely, I understood how much his job meant to him, and so I said that it was all right.

For the next week, things went on virtually just the same as they had on my first day. The only thing that changed was the menu. Stella visited daily and Edward came to see me when his business schedule allowed. My reasoning for his lack of visits, was put down to the fact he feared something may go wrong and while he engrossed himself in business he would worry less about our baby.

On Tuesday the twenty first of March 1967, after I had been in hospital for just over a week, my pain returned, the nurse called for the doctor. Not wanting to take any chances he advised me that he would perform a caesarean. I did not hesitate or question his recommendations, but signed the consent form and was wheeled to surgery. That afternoon I gave birth to a healthy baby girl, she was beautiful, all fingers and toes were perfect. She had a full head of hair just as Jake had and the biggest dimples I had ever seen on her chubby little face. Edward was telephoned when I went into surgery but did not show up until much later that evening due to a business meeting. I could sense that he was disappointed in not being able to show up earlier, especially, when he realised that Stella had beaten him to see his baby daughter.

She weighed seven pounds and two ounces and nothing I had ever seen before could be compared to her cuteness, especially when she poked her tongue out between her tiny lips. Both Edward and I were relieved that everything had turned out fine, although I did sense that maybe he was a little disappointed with not having a son.

We named her Claire, after a character in a movie I had once seen and had truly admired. I never forgot this characters name. For it was her courage, conviction, perseverance and drive to overcome seemingly impossible situations that I truly admired. She was also a caring person. I remembered comparing many of her qualities to those of Aunt Kate. I hoped my daughter would have those same attributes.

I stayed in hospital for just over a week, after giving birth to Claire; the doctor was still concerned with the level of my blood pressure and so as a precaution I agreed, with no complaints. Feeding time was so exciting for me; I would look forward to holding my little baby girl. Changing her nappies was a different story; I did not have a strong stomach when it came to smells, especially when it involved the smell of dirty nappies. Sometimes, I wondered if it would help if I wore a peg on my nose. Visually, things didn't effect me, blood, and guts, horrid sights no worries at all, it was just the smell.

By the time I was discharged from hospital, I was slowly adjusting to the smell. Although I never completely felt comfortable, I certainly got over the urge to vomit when I entered a room containing a dirty nappy.

Edward came and picked me up from the hospital, he had secretly been working on the nursery and I was pleasantly surprised at his wonderful results. A pink border with clowns and balloons ran around the room, it was very feminine. Edward stood inside the room with a grin from ear to ear, he was proud of his efforts and I was glad he had also focused some energy into his family life.

The world was changing greatly. In 1967, Aborigines were finally recognised as citizens of Australia. Up until then, they had been regarded as part of the Flora and

Fauna of Australia and were not able to participate in voting. These reforms I believed would only improve our nation, I was glad Claire was born into a world of improving times.

CHAPTER TWENTY-TWO

Soon after my arrival back home with Claire, Edward's hours at the office seemed to increase while the intimacy within our relationship decreased. The values, which we had once shared, were overruled by economic values, while his position within the company he worked, was always at the top of his priorities. As time went by, he became self absorbed. Work and money became even more important than they had before Claire's arrival. I had money, enough money to sustain a comfortable life, but Edward now seemed to resent this wealth. His old fashioned values made him feel that as a man it was his duty to support his family.

On Wednesday the eighth of May 1968, I received a telephone call from Edward's mother's neighbour. She had not seen or heard from his mother for a few days and had become concerned by the absence of his mother at bingo the night before. This was not the first time we had received a call of this nature. Mrs. Scott was a very nervous lady. However, unable to contact Edward, I decided that I should go over and check on his mother. As I drove into her driveway her neighbour Mrs. Scott met me on the verandah. She was a dear old lady who always knew the gossip of the street and made the most wonderful fruitcakes. She appeared nervous and was apprehensive about entering the house after no one had replied. Offering to hold Claire, she took a step back from the doorway, I slipped the key into the lock, turned it, then the handle and entered the house.

Inside, it was dark as the drapes were drawn shut and it took a while for my eyes to adjust. Straight before me was a hallway, as I looked down it I startled myself as I came face to face with my own reflection in the large mirror, which hung at the end. I exhaled deeply, regained my composure and took a step forward. To my left, there was the doorway to the lounge room, on my right a spare bedroom. Down at the end near the mirror the hallway branched out in both directions, to the left was the kitchen through to the laundry and to the right was the bathroom and another bedroom. As I proceeded into the lounge room, the floorboards creaked sending a chill through my body.

"Hello, are you there, hello, hello…" I repeated in a soft and unsure tone.

My eyes scanned the lounge room and I could not see Edward's mother. I stepped back into the hallway and next searched the front bedroom, this check did not take long to complete as Mrs. Rutherford was a hoarder and most of the space was occupied by piles of old furniture and boxes.Making my way back into the hallway near the front door, I heard Claire making her cute baby noises as Mrs. Scott whispered in asking, "Is everything alright dear?" I acknowledged by shaking my head and said that I still had to check through the rest of the house. "OK dear," she replied, "I will be right here if you need me."

I knew, she would not step a foot in the house, unless I emerged with Mrs. Rutherford and so I continued to make my way down the hallway. The kitchen was a little brighter than the rest of the house and it was the next room I searched, followed by the laundry.

Turning around I headed back to the hallway; next,

I would have to search the bedroom and finally the bathroom.I continued with calling.

"Hello, are you there, hello is anyone there?"

Entering the bedroom I expected to find Mrs. Rutherford in bed, but again, I could not see her anywhere. The bed covers had crinkles in them as if someone had been lying on top of the bed. I walked in a little further and checked down beside the bed, as I could not see there from the door and feared Mrs. Rutherford may have fallen over. She was not there.

Exiting the room, I headed to the bathroom, the door was closed and I hesitated as I reached for the handle. Slowly I pulled down on the handle and gently pushed the door open. An overpowering and vile smell hit me in the face and I gasped for air. Flinging my right hand over my mouth, I tried to refrain from gagging everywhere. Something was rotten inside the bathroom yet, I could not see what as the door was only half open. I suspected it was Mrs. Rutherford but had to be sure and so with my right hand covering my nose and mouth, I pushed the door open fully with my left hand and proceeded inside.

There she was. In the bath. By the look of her body, she had been there for some time. I had never seen the body of a person who had been dead for a period of time. She was all blue and puffy, so much so that at first I doubted it was her. Again, I felt as though I would gag. The stench was nearly unbearable. I had never smelt anything like it in my life. Nothing compared to the ghastly stench. I stepped backwards and nearly tripped over the bath towel, which lay on the floor. For a second I thought I was going to end up in the bath with her. Grabbing the basin I quickly recovered my composure and yelled to Mrs. Scott that she should call an ambulance.

Mrs. Scott yelled back inside asking me if her friend was all right to which I replied, "No, Mrs. Scott, no, I think you should maybe wait for me, don't call the ambulance." I closed the bathroom door and made my way back up the hallway and out to the verandah, where I gasped for fresh air. My skin was clammy and as I sat on the front step, I looked at my hands to see them tremble. For a moment I sat there, again trying to regain my composure, Mrs. Scott fussed around me asking me if I would be all right and told me that I was white as a ghost.

After a quiet moment, I heard her weeping. It was then; that she realised Mrs. Rutherford was dead. She had lost her lifetime friend and so I helped her to sit down on the step fearing if I did not, she would fall down.

There was no use going back inside. I closed the front door and we made our way over to Mrs. Scott's where I telephoned for an the ambulance and White's funeral home. Then, I telephoned Edward to tell him of his mother's death. At first when I called his secretary, she said that he was in a meeting and he could not be disturbed. I saw red and raised my voice telling her I did not care if he was in the most important meeting of his life or just having a cup of coffee. Then, I demanded to speak to my husband, advising her I had just found his mother dead. A click was the next thing I heard. I hoped that his secretary had not disconnected the telephone call. Edward answered the telephone in a huff. I could tell he was upset by the news of his mothers' death and that he had been disturbed. His initial response being, "Damn not now, why now?" then he informed me that he would be at his mothers as quickly as possible. After I hung up the telephone, I wondered what he was more upset about, his mother's death or the timing of my telephone call.

Over the last year, his personality had changed so much that I wondered if he was in fact the same man I married or an imposter.

I heard his car, as he drove up the street and into his mother's drive. Before I had a chance to get outside of Mrs. Scott' s house Edward had made his way into his mother's house. He too, would see the gruesome discovery and within moments, he emerged from the house just as I had gasping for breath. I sat with him on the front step, my arm around his shoulder and waited for the funeral directors to arrive. Mrs. Scott held onto Claire, it was not the place for a little baby to be so she kept her on her front lawn.

Edward was in shock. Looking at me with mournful eyes, he questioned why he had not made more time to see his mother. He blamed himself for her being abandoned in the coldness of the bath water, for what appeared to be days. An ambulance soon arrived followed by a car from the funeral home. We chatted briefly before two of the ambulance officers went into the house to collect the body. They had grown accustomed to seeing dead people and did not seem at all deterred by our description of Edward's mother. Placing rubber gloves on their hands they walked into the house and headed down the hallway to the bathroom carrying a stretcher.

When they had removed her body we closed the front door, collected Claire from Mrs. Scott's and drove home. I instructed Edward to follow me, he was an emotional mess and I did not want him driving through a red light or stop sign. Claire giggled in the back of the car; she was oblivious to the events, protected by her young age. As we drove home, I kept glancing in the rear vision mirror just to ensure Edward was still behind.

The funeral was held on the following Monday, an autopsy revealed she had died of natural causes. Although, I never doubted it would reveal anything more. Mrs. Scott travelled with us in the funeral car, Stella came over and insisted that she take Claire for the day and I gladly accepted her offer.

Although, I was fond of Mrs. Rutherford, at the funeral I could not shed a tear for her. I did cry. Actually, you could probably say I was carrying on like a blubbering idiot. Instead of tears for Mrs. Rutherford, they were tears for the loss of my parents, Bugsy, my grandma, Aunt Kate and little Jake. As every moment passed, my thoughts of them changed.

My parents had been gone for nearly thirty years and I could not make them come back. I could not change anything that had happened. I was only fifteen when they disappeared. Bugsy, he had been gone for over twenty-five years. He had his life stolen at such a young age. He was my knight in shining armour and left me when I was only eighteen. He was only twenty-one. Next, I had endured the loss of my grandma who in my heart I had loved dearly but sadly I had never had the opportunity to express this love due to the unknown distance between us. I still wished it had been possible to have been closer to her. Aunt Kate, my loving Aunt Kate, she had left me nearly four years ago. I could not believe how fast time had gone by. Then, there was little Jake he had entered this world for such a brief moment, over two years ago. Not a day went by, without one of the six entering my thoughts.

When the funeral was over and all the guests had

left our house, Edward and I went for a stroll in the garden. As we sat by the edge of the pond Edward broke down. He was feeling guilty for his long hours in the office and lack of family time and so he vowed he would change. I welcomed his change, he would arrive home at a reasonable time and he showed an interest in Claire, like I had never seen before. The imposter who had once taken possession of my husband's body was gone, the man I fell in love with had returned.

One week after Mrs. Rutherford's funeral, Stella telephoned and asked if she could come over for a visit. This request in itself was not unusual, however, she explained that she needed to talk and tell me something in person. Immediately, I feared the worst, maybe she had cancer or a terminal illness. I braced myself for what was to follow, pacing the house as I awaited her arrival.

Approaching the front door, Stella had a spring in her step. I was confused; her actions were not those of a dying person. My thoughts were not facts; they were far from it. Opening the door Stella greeted me with a huge hug; there was no doom and gloom. Taking my hand Stella led me to the lounge and without any further delays she blurted out "I've met someone Shirley, I've met someone who is so special." I was stunned, I hadn't seen Stella this happy in years. I was relieved, happy and excited and so I demanded she tell me more.

Stella explained that she had met Sam while viewing an art exhibition. Instantly, there was an attraction and when the two had struck up a conversation she had felt a special connection, a familiarity, a comfort and feeling of belonging that things were as they were meant to be. The only issue that may be viewed as negative, was that for Stella to follow her heart she would be moving to

Melbourne. As Stella sat next to me holding my hand and describing Sam her words exuded love, descriptions of beautiful eyes, a gorgeous smile, the instant attraction, the feeling of oneness, being oblivious of others around them. It was clear Stella was in love. Many people can search their entire lives looking for love, sadly some never find it, and unfortunately for others they lose it and never get a second chance. Stella had found it, she had a second chance and there was no way I could doubt or question it. I shared in her happiness and extended my best wishes.

Stella explained she would be leaving Sydney by the end of the week. There was no time like the present and before she left she wanted for me to meet Sam then I would be able to see with my own eyes what a special person Sam was.

The following Saturday we met for coffee, Stella was ready to leave, clutching Sam's hand as we made our way to the table, sharing affectionate glances and holding hands across the table I witnessed the love Stella had described. Whilst I was sad at Stella leaving. I could not begrudge her chance at happiness.

Hugging each other, we said our farewells. It was an emotional time, tears represented sadness and joy, loss and hopes. Placing her hands gently on my cheeks, Stella looked into my eyes and said, "We are today the creation from what we were yesterday, the day before yesterday and all the days before that. We are a product moulded by our environment and those who have entered our lives. I would not be the person I am today if it weren't for you and the past we share. I love you and I thank you for assisting me in being the person I am today."

Stella was gone and so we would continue our

friendship living miles apart, communicating over the telephone and with letters.

Edward's change was short lived, by Christmas he had reverted to being a work obsessive husband. It was obvious he had gotten over his guilt of not being around and for a short period of time he appeared more confident within himself due to the inheritance he received through the sale of his mothers house.

CHAPTER TWENTY-THREE

On Christmas day, Edward spent the morning with Claire and I, before he retreated to his study. I was furious; Claire was at an age when he should have been devoting more of his time to her. She was just starting to walk around and talk.

By the time Australia Day arrived, I began to suspect Edward might have been having an affair. However, I did not have any tangible evidence. When I confronted him with my suspicions he adamantly denied my allegations and said that, I had offended him. I could not help but suspect something, when he came home; he began to smell differently, he looked and talked differently. Were these only figments of my imagination resulting from my paranoia that things could not remain happy, or were these signs that things were really going from bad to worse at an uncontrollable rate?

We had been married for three years. Claire was two and Edward was changing, pulling further and further away from us both. I also wondered if he resented me for the loss of our son. He did not say as much, but I could sense he might have by the little things he would say.

I tried to talk to Edward, yet, he would not acknowledge he had a problem, nor admit our relationship was suffering due to the long hours he spent in the office. His dismissive attitude became hard to bear, not to mention the attitude that followed him inside the house. When I spoke about future plans he became ambiguous and this only acerbated the situation, I could not help but feel my marriage was spiralling downwards. I was headed for another disaster.

On Monday the twenty first of July 1969, I sat frozen in awe on my lounge, my eyes glued to the television as I watched the first men land on the moon. The flag may have been American, but it was a moment that belonged to us all. Many older people refused to accept such a feat, claiming it to be a hoax, an elaborate stunt using trick camera work and props. It proved hard for the elderly to accept the changing world, to accept man in the depths of space. They had travelled as far as the eye could see in the night sky yet the distance between them and the rest of the world could not compare to the isolation I felt. Outside my front door people walked by, people continued with their lives, they chatted and exchanged pleasantries. It was only inside my house and within my life, I experienced a loneliness and isolation. Edward and I had not spoken for over a week.

It was time I took control of my life; time I stopped worrying about Edward and started to concentrate on Claire and myself. I resigned myself to the fact he would not change; I could not change him especially if he would not admit there was a problem. Rather than trying to keep Claire awake until her father returned home after work as I had in the past, I commenced a daily routine that would have her in bed by seven o'clock. From then on, this routine resulted in Claire seeing her father less; Edward continued with his long hours and appeared oblivious to the change.

Claire was growing up so fast, her counting ability; recognition of colours, basic pictures and basic body parts was well advanced by the time she reached three. She was my beautiful little girl and it gave me great delight to see her all dressed up in her little frilly dresses. Before I knew it, she would be going off to school where her knowledge would be expanded and her personality would develop. For the time being, I spent nearly every waking hour with her, showing her all the wonderful things our world could offer. I wanted to protect her for as long as I possibly could; I did not want my little girl to be exposed to all the wrong in the world. I wanted her to have a life far better than I had. By talking to her and educating her from a young age I hoped she would be strong enough to stand up for her own rights and wise enough to know that although you may not agree with everything, as people we must learn to accept. Had my parents educated me in the same fashion then I am sure I would have turned out a different person, a better person.

I was one of many women influenced by Germaine Greer, who was the author of, The Female Eunuch, a book which encouraged all women to stand up for what they believed in, to stand up for their rights. She believed all women should be proud and independent and as I read the pages of her book, I felt my confidence build and a sense of pride fill my body.

The Women's Liberation movement was in full swing; the 1970's were a time of change. Before I knew it, Claire was off to her first day of school. As we walked to the school, Claire had excitement in her voice. She was going to meet many other children, make new friends and have heaps of fun. Skipping ahead of me she turned and said, "Mummy, I gunna have fun today and when you pick me up I gunna tell you everything I did." I smiled at her and said, "Yes sweetie, you are going to have a lot of fun." She turned and continued to merrily skip down the street. As we turned the corner with the schoolyard in view, Claire came to a sudden halt, it was then her unfamiliar surroundings and the thought she would be abandoned scared her. When I caught up with her she grabbed my hand and squeezed it.

"I don't wanna go, mummy, but I don't want you to leave me."

I stopped and knelt down before her, she had tears in her eyes and her bottom lip was trembling.

"You are going to have so much fun sweetie and I will be here waiting for you in the afternoon."

She did not seem to be too convinced by my words, but never the less when I rose to my feet she hesitantly continued walking by my side.

The schoolyard was filled with teary-eyed children and many teary-eyed parents. Taking your child to school for the first day was more emotional than I would have ever imagined. Finally, I was introduced to her kindergarten teacher and when the bell rang I wiped her eyes and said my farewell, promising to be outside when she finished that afternoon. And I was, children flooded out the classroom door all anxiously scanning the playground for their parents. Claire was one of the first out, in her hand she held a painting. When she made it to my side she grabbed my hand and asked if she could go back again tomorrow, it was obviously a successful day. The walk home was filled with stories of her day, friends she had made, games they had played, stories they had read and plans her teacher had in store for the next day.

Time proved that Claire enjoyed school. She was learning so much and making many friends. I recall during the first years of her schooling when I asked her what she did at school and she would reply, "Oh, we played, just played." School was like one big learning game. Friends would come over after school and on weekends. Claire was an extrovert, and she was the leader of her group, an organiser. I would hear them outside in the backyard playing, Claire giving instructions or explaining different topics they had learnt at school. I had converted the old garden shed into a cubby house. I wanted Claire to enjoy her childhood, so that one day when she reflected over her life she would be able to smile as she reminisced. Extending upwards on the garden shed proved successful, rarely did children have such a large cubby house, let a lone a two story one. Downstairs was a play area, which contained many toys and an old lounge while upstairs there was a bed, table and chairs. It was her own private getaway where she could entertain friends. The view from the upstairs window took in the entire backyard including the pond, while having it fitted with electricity meant her entertaining would not stop at night fall.

During the warmer months, Claire's friends would join us for barbecues. I was always happy for friends to visit, as I knew they bought so much joy to her life. Being an only child as I was, I did not want Claire to experience loneliness.

After nightfall, they would play a game called "spotlight." One child would perch themselves in the upstairs window with a bright torch trying to spot the others who daringly would try to sneak up on the cubby house without being seen. From the kitchen window I would watch figures scamper from one safety zone to another. The torch beam would whiz around the backyard, while echoes of laughter filled the air until finally a loud yell would symbolise someone had been spotted out or made it back to the cubby house without being seen.

Edward continued his long hours at the office; occasionally he would attend school functions although he always failed to possess the same excitement I felt.

Claire participated in many school plays, her first and indeed the most memorable was when she was in second class, where she played the part of Grumpy one of the seven dwarfs. It was to be an adaptation of Snow White; into a musical but as the performance transpired what resulted was a mixture of both music and comedy. Sleepy walked himself off the front of the stage. Snow White was initially stunned by stage fright and had to be prompted with her lines from behind the curtains. While to make matters worse the apple intended for Snow White had to be replaced with a banana after it was eaten by little Johnny Jackson the walking disposal unit who suffered a serious case of nerves and got the munchies. The performance was awarded with a standing ovation and the evening was re-lived within many discussions even years later.

From the time, Claire turned six, Saturday mornings were reserved for little athletics, where she excelled in high jump and long distance running. Ribbons decorated her bedroom walls, while trophies were displayed on her dresser. She was openly proud of her achievements both athletic and academically, revelling in the praise she received. I wanted to give Claire all the love and support she could wish for. I wanted her to feel proud of whom she was. I did not want her to suffer from low self-esteem as I had in my life. She knew, as her mother I was always there for her. I encouraged her to voice her opinions, discussing topics in an open manner and answering her questions.

Time appeared to be flying by at an amazing rate; we were now preparing for her tenth birthday. She was in sixth class, next year she would be heading off to high school; my baby girl would soon be a young woman. We had been planning a party for over one month; Claire wanted a theme party and a sleepover. Three weeks before the party Claire wrote the invitations and handed them out at school. Edward promised that he would be there but I did not hold my breath. He had a habit of making promises only to break them.

Claire and I decorated the house with streamers and balloons; party food covered the dining room table along with party hats and whistles. Claire had started to play the violin and so on the morning of her birthday I made a violin cake, then I got busy wrapping the "pass the parcel" and hiding lollies for the treasure hunt. The party commenced at two o'clock and children arrived in droves. I was not sure how I would possibly manage twelve giggling girls but in the end, I did manage and all enjoyed the sleepover.

Edward arrived home when all the festivities were over; again, he missed the cake and the singing of happy birthday. Again, he had let our daughter down.

That was the final straw, I could not continue in the habits of this marriage. We had not acted like a husband and wife for years, we were more like two individuals sharing the same house, our paths crossing spasmodically.I no longer believed we should stay together for the sake of Claire. I did not want her exposed to the unhappiness I was enduring, the unhappiness that was surely affecting her. Time had showed me that it alone could not heal our relationship or a feeling only we could, that was the biggest misconception of my life, that time heals. Time does not heal, people do.

I did not want Claire to suffer the painful and everlasting effect of divorce; in those days I knew no one who was divorced or who was getting a divorce. With butterflies in my stomach I approached Edward and told him I wanted a divorce. Surprisingly enough, he took my request well and without hesitation he agreed, he also agreed it would be better if he purchased a place of his own and moved out as soon as possible. I was stunned, for years he had not admitted there was a problem. Yet, on the first opportunity he had he was only too happy to jump ship.

Edward and I divorced in 1978; we were lucky that new laws had been introduced making it easier. Previously couples had to go to court and give statements detailing why the marriage failed also there had to be a partner blamed for the demise. All we had to do was to prove we had been separated for twelve months.

Edward's leaving had a devastating effect on Claire, for years she had accepted that her father was a busy man, but now her father would no longer come home. The initial effect was shattering, it was like death, so much hatred and anger, a lot of tears and questions; where is my daddy? I did not want Claire to feel trapped between Edward and myself. There was no way that Edward would ever make me feel threatened or insecure by the time he spent with his daughter. Claire and I shared a bond, which I had not shared with my mother, nothing would come between us and so I encourage her to visit her father. I had to allow her to love her father, although my love for Edward had disappeared. It was not her divorce; she was an innocent victim, entitled to love both parents without criticism from either one.

I was amazed at how many people came forward with their opinions and reasons for our failed marriage. Most had not experienced any such thing, but miraculously knew only too well the reasons behind our family breakdown. If only they had shut their mouths and minded their own business then I believe our separation may have been a little kinder to all concerned. No one has the right to point fingers at those experiencing divorce. Especially those who have never lived under the same roof or who have only been privy to part of the story. There are always two sides of the story; there is always more than one casualty in a divorce.

With time, Claire began to understand she had not been a contributing factor for our separation, she continued to live with me, regularly seeing her father, loving us both equally. By the time she was a teenager, it was clear that Claire resented all those who had stood back pointing fingers of blame during our separation.

I could understand this resentment but as her mother, I did not want her to hold onto negative feelings. Taking her hand, I said to her, "As humans we are all capable of making mistakes, of hurting those around us. But, we must be capable of admitting when we have made mistakes and also be able to forgive those who make mistakes - nobody is perfect."

Not one of the finger pointers, admitted to doing any wrong.

CHAPTER TWENTY-FOUR

Claire was fifteen and her birthday like many others was celebrated with another sleepover. As she sat at the breakfast table, I studied her face. She was so gentle and forgiving, maybe a little precocious for her age, yet nothing like I was when I was fifteen. I prayed her life would turn out better than mine, that she would not make the same mistakes that I had when I was younger. Although, she was alive when the Vietnam War occurred, she had been much too young to have this affect her life and the way in which she viewed the world. This thought gave me relief.

Time had passed at an amazing rate, as mother and daughter we shared so many experiences.

Her sleepover guests arrived just after lunch. I was happy with her group of friends; so many children of her age had no idea of their future and appeared to wander around like lost souls. Yet, most of Claire's friends had their sights clearly focused on a good education and careers to follow. There were ten that were planning to sleep over. All of them were very much individuals and despite the mixture of family and cultural back grounds. All of them accepted each other and grew from each other's individuality.

Two of her friends who stuck most clearly in my mind were the Hoffman twins. They were identical in appearance, although their personalities could not have been more different. It amazed me that they were able to socialise within the same circle of friends. Emotionally within, I was sure they shared a love for each other like no individual could share without first being a twin. Although, there always appeared to be a friction between them. This friction had always been evident even from a young age when I was first introduced. I could only imagine what it would have been like to continually be compared to another, to continually have to strive for your own individuality and your own place in life while constantly being compared to another. I would imagine that after a while and as you matured, you may resent the other. For you, as an individual would feel you could never truly be who you wanted to be without being judged against another who for biological reasons looked the same.

I had such a great interest in the twins. I remember I once spoke to a friend of Edward's who was a psychologist about them. He had undertaken studies into the behaviour of twins and their relationships. What he told me totally amazed me; he said sometimes when twins are in the first stages of creation even before the egg is split there is so much friction within the cells, this friction results in the splitting. It was like ying and yang, black and white. Both can not survive together, both are very much opposite. When a split results under these conditions, it is unlikely neither will get along in life. The turmoil experienced within the womb is never forgotten. Child hood experiences and family life keep them together at a young age, the security of one another. However, as adolescence approaches, generally each will go their separate way. One, generally the younger, is often viewed as the weaker of the two and this weakness in many cases turns into jealousy and resentment. Even if outsiders do not view the younger as the weaker, this feeling is carried by the individual and they generally harbour resentment towards the older twin. I wondered if Christine, the younger of the two actually did feel resentment and jealousy or if, in fact, it was just a theory. I would never dare ask the question, upsetting Claire's friends was not on my agenda. I wanted her to view me as not only her mother but also a friend. Pizza and Kentucky Fried Chicken, delivered to the door, were on the dinner menu. Not exactly the healthiest of choices, yet, convenient and pleasing to all. Fast foods had infiltrated our society creating laziness and a population full of overweight people.

It was great to see Claire so happy and so comfortable within herself. Pillows and blankets covered the lounge room floor, bodies everywhere. From the kitchen, I gathered drink orders listening to the conversations. Most of the time it was difficult to make out the content of their discussions, a room full of adolescent girls trying to have their voices heard was nearly impossible. I shook my head and chuckled to myself, wondering if the videos they had hired would be watched or if the entire night would be consumed with chatter. Through out the ages the topics discussed by adolescent girls may have changed slightly, yet, I was sure the enthusiasm behind them would never alter.

Eventually, the videos were played, however, by the time the first minutes of the second video were playing most had assumed comfy positions and closed their eyes. By the time midnight arrived, all were fast asleep and so I turned it off and went to bed. In the morning the sound of chatter downstairs woke me and so I decided it would be best to venture down and see what the consensus was for breakfast plans. Eleven hungry teenage girls in your kitchen with no supervision could result in an unsightly mess or a cooking disaster.

Bacon, scrambled eggs and toast were the orders on the day, from all except for one friend Jessie. With suggestions flying across the kitchen Jessie turned her nose in the air and began to express her unhappiness about the idea of bacon and eggs stating quite firmly that she would have nothing. Not wanting an unhappy guest and with Jessie looking like the kind of girl who preferred sweeter delicacies I suggested pancakes with jam or maple syrup. A wise choice, no sooner had the word pancake left my mouth that Jessie proclaimed in a loud voice, "I love pancakes," and so I proceeded with the preparations and cooking.

They were all so full of dreams of the future, as I cooked and listened, I wished I could grant them all their dreams. I wished that their trouble free lives would remain just that, trouble free. They were so young and so innocent, so full of life and energy.

My personal life took a back seat. I was not interested in meeting anyone. My priority, was the welfare of my daughter.

In the years that followed Claire's schooling, study and mixing with her friends consumed our lives. Claire met and fell in love with her first boyfriend, Brian, when she was sixteen. He was a tall and honest boy, kind hearted and very easy going. Their relationship lasted just over two years, the separation amicable and only due to Brian's work commitments taking him inter-state. Claire was devastated, although they remained in contact.

Brian was Claire's first love and she missed his caring presence. Brian too was very upset with their parting; I had grown to look upon him as part of our family. Birthdays and special occasions were celebrated together, while many deep and meaningful conversations took place over our dinner table. With Brian around, our house possessed a loving and caring atmosphere, pranks and jokes, laughter and understanding. Brian assured me that his intentions were nothing less than honourable, he had a great respect for both Claire and me and so I trusted in his words. He never disappointed me or abused this trust. The day he left I found a letter from him in our letterbox, although brief in content, it held great meaning and would never be forgotten.

Dear Shirley,

I am sure you can appreciate the difficulty in my having to say goodbye and therefore I wish you only the very best life can offer. Since being with Claire; the places I have seen, the events and people I have met all combined together have produced a recipe for the best time I have experienced within my life. I am sure without any one of these ingredients, things would not have been the same. That includes the opportunity I had to meet you. Now I have wonderful memories to last a lifetime. Thank you for the kindness you offered and the wisdom you shared. Again, I wish you only the very best for the future.

Kind regards
Brian Long

I found comfort in the thought of knowing I could influence upon another life, in such a positive way and although I shed tears while reading his words I felt happiness and satisfaction in this fact.

When Claire and Brian first met, I thought fate would see them together for the rest of their lives. They appeared so well matched, so in love, yet, love itself could not keep them together. The forces, which drive our universe, had other ideas for them both.

Many of us, have tried to understand how the forces of nature work, numerous theories have been studied. Yet, the real reason behind why things happen could never be known. It was impossible, things they say happen for a reason, and I could not begin to imagine the reasons behind many things. Maybe, this discovery would only be made after death. I believe we all have to experience a certain degree of sadness, of trying and hard times so that we can clearly appreciate good. However, as far as anything else goes, your guess would be as good as mine.

Studying for her Higher School Certificate proved stressful. Claire placed high expectations upon her academic achievements. These expectations combined with her teachers constantly reiterating that the rest of their lives balanced on examination results, plus peer pressure, resulted in drastic weight loss. At first, jumpers and jackets, baggy clothes camouflaged the reduction in her weight. It was only as the weather warmed up and Claire shed the layers of clothing, that the shocking change in her physical appearance was noticed. Months before I had questioned her eating habits. Study group locations were rotated between friends' houses. Some nights I would feed several study companions, while on other nights the house would remain silent. Claire assured me she was looking after herself and so my concerns were eased. It was my belief that foods along with facts were being consumed elsewhere, but that had not always been the case. Confronting the issue again Claire acknowledged her weight loss and told me her initial loss resulted from skipping the occasional meal. However, as time passed and her workload increased her eating desires decreased. I was lucky, my daughter was honest, and our relationship was very open, together we instigated a plan to improve her diet and put some balance back into her life. Within days of introducing a balanced study, eating and sleeping regime, Claire noticed an increase in her attention span and memory retention abilities. We all survived the Higher School Certificate and came out the other end stronger and wiser individuals. Claire's results were amongst the top ten percent in New South Wales and I was a very proud mother.

CHAPTER TWENTY-FIVE

A young lady stood before me. It was Claire. No longer a girl, she had blossomed into a beautiful young lady. Edward and I had met and agreed on celebrating her eighteenth birthday with a large party. He was capable of being pleasant when we were alone but became childish when surrounded by friends and family, always keeping his distance. I could not understand this behaviour; he had nothing to be afraid of with me. Both of us were content with our new separate lives. There was no way I would ever think of rekindling the relationship. Not even in my wildest dreams. My only hopes were to be friendly and civil, to act as two mature adults, no matter who was around. I knew only too well that the past was the past, there was nothing that could be done to change events.

Claire agreed to the party we suggested. Throughout her life she had met so many people and made new friends. Her list of guests exceeded fifty; many were friends she had met while at school, and others she had met at different social events. Edward and I were happy to split the cost; the most important thing was that Claire should celebrate her birthday in a way, which would make her happy. In the end, it was decided that the party would be held at home. This way we could monitor the alcohol consumption and make sure that the only guests who were there were those who had received an invitation. Too many times, we had heard of other parties being crashed by undesirables and so we decided to employ the services of a security guard that would check invitations and allow entry.

The street out front was filled with cars, the backyard was decorated with lanterns and a large marquee was erected to house the main eating area and dance floor. Claire's main concern was the entertainment and so we hired a local Sydney band that for a reasonable price played a variety of music into the early hours of the morning.

Month's prior to her birthday, Claire had asked if it would be possible to have a car for her birthday. She had mentioned buying a car for over a year, since she had obtained her driving license and had been saving her pocket money. Many of her older friends owned their own cars, Claire wanted to feel included within her peers and be capable of offering lifts when they went out. Previously, she would borrow my car or on occasion, she would use Edward's. Finally, a week before her birthday Edward agreed to Claire's request, she would receive a small second-hand car from us both. The only criteria it had to fill was, not too old, not too big and not too powerful. It was a little red Corolla, just something to get her from A to B. Claire was ecstatic when we handed her the keys, never in her wildest dreams did she imagine that her wish would come true. Hugging us both we made her promise that she would drive sensibly, that she would never drink and drive and that she would take full responsibility for the fuel, insurance and registration. For those few seconds we were both her heroes'.

Partygoers arrived in droves; they ate, drank, danced and sung to their hearts content. To my surprise, there was no sign of trouble, I was so pleased, my wish for a trouble free night had come true. The band stopped playing at two in the morning, by that time many of the younger guests were organising where the celebrations would move. In Sydney, the night was still young and bars would be open till the sun came up. By three in the morning the backyard was empty, those guests who had been drinking had telephoned taxis, others car-pooled. The party was a huge success and our baby girl, who was no longer a baby, was out and about continuing with her party and friends.

Surprisingly, Edward offered to stay back and help me clear up some of the mess. He had been drinking a little and for once, he was very approachable and friendly. Clearing the rubbish from the tables, we talked as if we had not talked in years, both of us were proud of Claire. If nothing else had been achieved out of our being together, we could both be happy for the daughter we had created. As we cleared the tables I looked at Edward, I knew he still cared about me, as I cared about him. It was just that over time, our being in love with each other had disappeared. Edward was very old fashioned, I think that is why he appeared to hold a grudge against me, when we were in the company of others. Maybe, not so much that he was angry with me, but more so, that he was angry about the fact our marriage had failed. Edward was never accepting of failure. But then again, not many people would marry if they knew their marriage was ultimately destined for failure. If that were the case, most would not even take the first step in having a serious relationship. No one wants to set themselves up for heartbreak, we all, even if only in a small part, believe in happily ever afters.

Once the rubbish was cleared away, I invited him in for quiet drink. There was a large amount of food and cake left and so we carried it into the kitchen where we sat and drank coffee reminiscing over the years, which we had spent together. I could see in his eyes the disappointment he felt when I discussed our daughter's life. There were so many areas he had missed due to his work commitments; these were precious moments, which could never be recovered. I think it was only over the cups of coffee on that night that Edward realised how much he had missed. I felt sad for Edward, I was sorry that he had missed out on so many irretrievable moments, sorry that no matter what I had said so many years ago fell on deaf ears. He was a caring father, his biggest problem was his career. He was so caught up in the world of business, that around him, so many things were passing unnoticed.

Edward let his work consume his life; he lived to work whereas most people work to live.

By the time, Edward decided to leave, the sun was coming up. Our conversation had lasted over three hours; it was an amazing night. Claire made it home just as Edward was leaving; she too had endured a very big night. Although she was upright, she was very much suffering the effects of alcohol as she slurred her words. Along with her arrival were two of her closest friends Jessie and Claudia. Jessie had been a long time friend; she had been in the same classes as Claire since kindergarten. Claudia had moved into the area when they started High School. Both girls were very responsible and although all were intoxicated I was happy knowing they would look after each other when they went out and ensure they all arrived home safely.

CHAPTER TWENTY-SIX

It was a sad occasion, when my daughter Claire came to me advising that she was moving out. I could understand that she had to leave home and live her own life. Every bird eventually flies the coop. Nevertheless, this knowledge did not displace the dejection I felt. My baby girl was now twenty, no more a baby. She was wise, independent, responsible, caring and strong enough to stand on her own two feet, to take on the world head on with all it had to offer.

Claire had been in a relationship with a handsome young man, Anthony, for the past year. It was time for her to take the next step and so she was moving out and in with him. I wished Claire all my best wishes, offered her some motherly advice and told her that my door would always be open should she need to come home.

Edward was also happy for Claire. Although, he was more critical of her moving out and was concerned, she would end up single and pregnant. Edward had old-fashioned values and did not share the confidence I had in Claire's decisions. I respected my daughter and loved her unconditionally. When I was younger, I had not possessed such abilities. Now that I was older and wiser, I had learned the importance of these qualities.

Claire did not end up single and pregnant, Anthony proposed to her after they had been living together for just less than two years. Not wanting to rush into their wedding, they set the wedding date for early 1991 and began making arrangements. As Claire discussed her ideas with me, I recalled the excitement I had felt when I had been making similar arrangements over twenty-five years ago. Her face displayed a constant smile, she was ecstatic and madly in love with Anthony. I was happy for her, I was glad Claire's life was turning out better than mine. At Claire's age, the only feelings that I possessed were dark and dismal, guilt and loneliness, despair and remorse. At her age, I did not dream of the future, I dwelled on the past.

Claire's wedding day soon arrived. Throughout the service, I wept tears of overwhelming joy. Claire was a beautiful bride and I was a proud mother.

Life continued on much the same, as it had before Claire's wedding after the celebrations were over. Both Anthony and Claire would visit on a regular basis; they had purchased a house at Waterloo. I had given them twenty thousand dollars as a wedding present. To Anthony it was a large amount and at first, he appeared embarrassed and hesitant to take it.Eventually, I won out and he accepted the money assuring me that it would not be wasted, it was the money they used as a deposit on their house. I was so happy to see them starting out on the right foot. I had plenty of money still sitting in the bank and was glad some of it could be put to a good use. Originally, I had planned to buy them a house as a wedding present, but then I reconsidered. By giving them enough for a deposit, they would learn the responsibility of paying off a house.

I had never had such a responsibility, my parent's house still stood vacant, I could not bear to live there with all its memories, yet, I could not part with it either. And so, I always maintained its appearance, while I lived in Aunt Kate's house. I had never had to work and sometimes I wondered if I had really missed one of the biggest experiences a person has in their life - saving for, then buying their first house. I was sure it would have created a certain degree of stress but the satisfaction of making the final payment would have been a wonderful experience, a great feat.

Claire did not know about my parent's house, her grandparent's house, no one knew. The knowledge of its existence died with Bugsy, my grandma, Aunt Kate and Stella. I did have other living relatives; however, as the house was never mentioned I presumed they thought it had been sold off years ago. I could never bear to sell it, it was my family home, my parents house. It represented so much to me although I had never stepped one foot inside since leaving, it was my parents' house and would always remain my parents' house. When Claire was about six she asked me about her grandparents. Rather than go into the whole story I told her that they had died in an accident. Although she was young, I could tell she sensed it was a painful topic and so from then on, she asked no more questions.

I probably should have told Claire the truth when she was older, but then it would only bring more questions. I had a hard enough time dealing with the situation and I wanted to protect my daughter from the pain I felt so the words never left my lips.

Anthony and Claire came to visit me around November 1992. They both had a grin from ear to ear and were bubbling with excitement. Claire was seventeen weeks pregnant. For the last few months, she had been suffering with a severe case of morning sickness. Both had just returned from the doctors, where they had had the first ultrasound. Claire produced the picture the doctor had given them and pointed out the baby's face, telling me it was a face only a mother could love. I too, had experienced the same excitement during my pregnancies and understood her feelings. Claire knew of her brother Jake, she knew I worried about her sickness and she assured me that the doctor was happy with the development of their baby.

By the time Christmas arrived, Claire had gained weight and her pregnancy could not go unnoticed. The baby was advancing well, many of its bones had begun to harden and the pads on its fingers and toes had developed finger and toe prints. Claire was a proud and healthy expectant mother; Anthony was a loving and supportive husband.

Claire gave birth to a healthy little boy on twenty-eighth of May 1993; I was the proud grandmother of Benjamin. His arrival made me feel old, I was old, I was sixty-nine and I worried that I would not see my grandson grow up to become a fine young man. Edward came to the hospital after Ben was born. He could not face being present for the birth, saying that he did not know if his stomach would handle it. By this time, Edward was retired, he had worked for the same company for over forty years. On his retirement, he left the position of managing director. He was more than just pleased with his achievements and I was glad that we had divorced all those years ago. Nothing was considered more important than his career and time had proven he would not have changed.

Edward had achieved a prestigious status within the business world and financial security. He had shares in the company he had worked for and a retirement package that would see him never wanting. I was happy for his success, but could not help but wonder if he had any regrets. He had missed sharing so many of our daughter's achievements.

Before I knew it, Benjamin turned one. We celebrated his birthday at Claire's house. Claire and Anthony wanted to make the occasion one that would be remembered so Anthony applied for a license and put on a mini fireworks display. Children from all over the neighbourhood watched from the street and joined in with singing happy birthday. Many were oblivious to whose birthday it was, but frolicked in the celebrations all the same. The fireworks preceded the birthday cake, which was shaped into the number one and had Pooh, Tigger and Piglet on it. As soon as the photos were taken and the candle was blown out, Benjamin reached over and before anyone had a chance to react, he had both hands squashing Pooh. Everyone laughed, no one had expected him to do such a thing, with birthday cake from ear to ear he sat in his high chair giggling with a cheeky grin on his face. By the end of the night, Benjamin was exhausted and fell asleep in my arms. As he lay there he looked like an angel, light reflecting on his fair hair shone as though it were a halo. He was an angel, he was my big angels little angel and I loved them both dearly.

With so many beaches and pools around the area, Claire decided she should take Ben to swimming lessons. She did not want her son to come to any harm. When I felt up to it I would join her at the pool, teaching children how to swim is always important. Although, I did not participate a great deal in the teaching, I found joy as I proudly watched my family blossom. Age was catching up with me. Although, I did not like to mention it, sometimes just the thought of walking down the street would make me tired. There were still so many things I dreamt of achieving in my life; sometimes I wondered if I had left too many things for far too long. I began to regret starting my family later in life, as this reduced the time I would possibly share in their lives. Hindsight is an amazing thing.

I had always dreamt of travelling to England and Europe, some of my father's relatives lived in England. It would have been nice to travel and discover where my father's family originated. For some unknown reason I had never made these trips, I had the money. I had the desire to go. Nevertheless, I never made the arrangements. I had always thought that I would do these things when I got older, when I had more personal time, after Claire left. However, when Claire left home, I discovered much of my confidence had also departed. The thought of travelling alone scared the hell out of me.

CHAPTER TWENTY-SEVEN

Dismal days are around me; the loneliness is so unbearable. As I sit in my recliner, I shudder with fear. Fear of the unknown. Fear of my future. Fear that all forms of happiness have gone forever. I have not received a visitor for over one month. The drapes are drawn. Rays of sunlight penetrate into the room between gaps in the drapes; yet, I can't summon the energy to venture out. Walking to the bathroom I pass the telephone and pick up the receiver just to verify it is still connected, it is. Why hasn't my daughter visited? Why has no one called, to see if I am all right? Have they all forgotten me?

In my loneliness, I question what my role in life is, where do I go from here? I am a mother and a grandmother, but is that all life has to offer. A title, a brief description of how I am to be represented within society.

In my younger years, I never gave much thought to the habits of elderly people; this is probably due to my limited interaction. Where did they all go, what did they all do after their families left home? Clean the house, potter around the garden. There is only so much gardening and pottering a person can do. Then there were activities such as lawn bowls, I could no further imagine flying to the moon than taking myself down to the local bowling green.

My life had been created through the years and now it was governed by the seasons. In summer, I would tend to the lawn and flowers, gardening in spring and sow in winter. Would my next real moment of happiness be experienced in my journey to the other side?

I tried to look at the positives, my health was better than many of my age, I had a roof over my head and I was far from the poverty line. I recalled a saying my father once said, so many years ago. He said, "Better to have half a loaf than no loaf at all." At the time, I looked at him puzzled and with that he said, "One day you will understand what I mean, one day, when you look at the world through adult eyes, things will appear so different." These words I never forgot and he was certainly correct in what he said, he was certainly correct.

Claire had been married for five years; Ben was already three years old. I had not seen them for five weeks and I missed them. Anthony's parents lived in New Zealand so they decided to take a holiday over there, but they should have been back last week. I tried to recall the dates Claire told me but could not remember. If I were correct in thinking, they would be home. All I knew was that I wished they were here. I wished I did not feel this intolerable seclusion.

At last, the telephone rang and it was Claire. I had been confused by the dates and she was phoning to tell me they had arrived home. She would be over in the morning to show me photos they had taken.Ben had also been asking about me, so she would be sure to bring him over as well.

They arrived at about morning teatime, so I prepared some drinks and set out biscuits and cake on a plate. Ben was at the age when he was inquisitive about everything. I could tell he was driving Claire crazy. He would ask a question, she would answer and then he would follow with another question or just, "Why?"I recalled Claire doing the same things when she was Ben's age and reassured her that he would soon go into another phase. It was a welcome relief to see them both. Ben and I strolled down to the pond, he enjoyed playing near the water edge and I was comforted by the fact I knew he would be able to swim if he happened to fall in. Claire relaxed on the banana lounge, while I joined in with Ben's game of make believe. He was a wonderful little boy who was not afraid of showing his emotions. Sitting on the soft grass by the water's edge he tugged on my sleeve, put both hands to his face cupping around his mouth and whispered, "I love you Nanna," then he gave me a gentle hug. I lent over and held Ben in my arms, "I love you too, sweetness." I had not heard nor spoken those three words for so many years. I felt a change, it was as if someone had turned on a light switch. Three simple little words made the world appear a brighter and happier place.

When it came time to return to the house, Ben helped me to my feet, as best he could. Together, we strolled across the lawn holding hands.

CHAPTER TWENTY-EIGHT

Claire arrived at my house at nine o'clock; I was still in my nightie and was sitting on the lounge having my morning cup of tea. I had phoned her the night before and asked that she accompany me to the doctors, he had requested that we have a family meeting. I was aware that my capabilities were not as good as they had once been. I would often find it difficult to complete basic tasks such as removing the lids from jars. The upstairs living area of my house had been left dormant for the last two years. After my fall, which resulted in a broken wrist, I lost a lot of self-confidence. From then on, I set myself up so I would reduce further injuries. Anthony and Claire had carried my bed downstairs to the lounge room. There it sat in the corner; two small wardrobes held enough clothes for every season, while separating my bedroom from the lounge and dining area. The closest I came to the upstairs area of the house was holding onto the banister rail support as I passed it on my way to the bathroom. Oh, how I had loved that banister rail in my younger years. When I touched it, I would remember the glee I experienced as I slid down from my bedroom and a tingling sensation would enter my body. There had not been many happy occasions in my younger years. Sliding down the banister rail meant more than just a quick route, it represented freedom. I would straddle the railing, close my eyes, inhale deeply, let go and then for a few seconds I would experience the same peace and freedom I imagined a bird would experience while soaring through the endless sky.

I assumed the doctor wanted to discuss my health and welfare. I thought that maybe, he would suggest home care or meals on wheels. Claire hurried me along, reminding me the appointment was for ten o'clock. Gulping down the last of my tea, I wanted to assure her even though I was old I had not forgotten how to tell the time, but I did not, instead I just shook my head and hurriedly got changed.

We made it to the doctor's surgery in plenty of time. Doctor Wijeratne had been my doctor for years and I had visited the surgery on numerous occasions. However, never before, had I noticed the antiseptic odour, which drifted out the door. I hesitated for a moment, until Claire took my arm and led me inside. Something inside me told me, that this visit would be like no other. I had not been sick, yet, doctor Wijeratne had also asked that Claire attend. There was a sound of movement in the surgery and I swallowed nervously, it was not Doctor Wijeratne that I was afraid of but what he might conclude from our meeting made me tremble with fear. It was too late; the surgery door opened and out emerged Doctor Wijeratne, white coat, grey hair and glasses, carrying a stethoscope around his neck.

Once we were in the surgery we took our seats, Doctor Wijeratne sat on the other side of his desk, and his face displayed a sense of concern and well being.

I had never really paid much attention to the layout of his office. However, as I sat in the chair, feeling as though I was again a schoolgirl who had been taken to the principal's office with my mother my eyes scanned the room nervously. His office was very spacious, a bookcase filled with books on nearly every medical topic you could imagine occupied an entire wall. Another wall was occupied by a bay window that looked out into a courtyard, gardens filled with daisies, roses and dahlias. The remaining wall space was painted with a very soft pastel blue. I grinned to myself, if someone had asked me what colour the room was before I had entered on that day I would not have been able to answer. Once I finished concentrating on the room around me I realised Claire and the doctor had been talking. She looked at me and for a second appeared quite annoyed, asking what was wrong she said, "You haven't been listening to a word we have been saying, have you?" Again, I felt as though I was a schoolgirl and she was the parent, I replied, "No," as I shrugged my shoulders.

Doctor Wijeratne had not wanted to discuss home care or meals on wheels; his approach to my situation was far more drastic. While, I had been examining the room, Claire and he had been discussing what they considered were suitable alternatives for housing.

After a lengthy discussion, it was agreed that I should accept my doctor's recommendations and move to a retirement village. In private, I was far from happy about the decision. I had been bombarded. Quietly, I wondered if this had not been an organised plot by Claire, to get rid of me.

Bitch! I thought. *How could she do this to me? How could she do this to her mother? Without me she would not be here,* as I thought this I also recalled how I had treated my mother.

I needed a reality check, perhaps it was time to make this move. I was seventy-four years old. Maybe her suggestions were only being made in the best interests of my welfare. My daughter was far from being as I was. The notion that she was sending me away to get rid of me, was crazy. Given that I had offered her only love and support throughout her life, the thought of her making this decision to place me in a retirement home just to get rid of me would have been ludicrous. Surely, such a thought would not enter her mind. The return trip home was very quiet; neither of us said a word. When we got into the lounge room Claire offered to make some lunch and a cup of tea. She could see the visit to the doctor had rattled me. She did not want to send me away and forget about me and so once lunch was eaten, we sat in the lounge room and discussed our options.

Finally, both of us agreed such a drastic step was not yet required. Since my moving downstairs, I had not suffered any major accidents. For now, the idea to move would be placed on hold, I had regained the majority of my self-confidence and while I felt capable of living alone that was how it would remain. As Claire left she extended her hand towards me and took hold of mine. She asked me to promise her that should I feel the need to revisit the idea I would tell her, other than that she said, "We will see how things go, maybe in six months we should re-assess our options." I nodded in acceptance; I could not force myself to acknowledge in words fearing that those words would also clearly acknowledge my deteriorating life.

At some stage, throughout our lives, many of us fear death. On many occasions I had prayed for death, I had viewed it as an escape. Now was the time in my life when I experienced the fear of death, the dying part did not worry me, it was what followed the dying that scared the hell out of me. Fear of the unknown. This fear had invaded my mind to such an extent that I offered the grandfather clock which stood in the hallway to Claire and Anthony.

I had once admired the beauty of this timepiece as they did. But now, its ticking simply represented the counting down of my life here on earth.

Autumn arrived so fast that year; it was as if one day I looked out the window and gazed at the summer heat reflecting off the roadway, people resting in the shade of the tree lined streets. Then the next morning, all the heat had disappeared, all trees had been stripped of their leaves. I was sure someone with much greater powers had turned the temperature gauge down and sent through a plague of locusts to remove the leaves.

Claire continued with her regular visits and gradually I reduced my trips outdoors. Until one day, as I sat on the lounge, I no longer recalled the last time I had stood beneath the sun. Smelt the sweet aroma of the flowers in the garden, felt the grass between my toes or gazed at the calming water in the pond. My time inside was continual. I envisaged the duration of my life being one of isolation. I had become somewhat like a hermit. The walls around me offered security and shelter, while at the same time they stole all hope of companionship and any form of social interaction. The majority of my time was spent sitting on the lounge watching useless garbage on the idiot box, yet time appeared to be passing by at an amazing rate.

My shelf life for this world appeared to be shortening with every blink of my eyes. It is a fact, that the human eye blinks about nine thousand, three hundred and sixty-five times a day. I was sure this was no longer the case for me. Every blink of my eyes no longer took a fraction of a second, my body was old and weary and I required regular naps to rest. Simple things, which had once required the slightest physical energy now, required great exertion. I was of sound mind and frustrated by my disabilities. Time had taken its toll on me physically, my legs would no longer do what my head wanted them to. My entire body ached and I was sure I could hear myself creaking.

I could not give in. Rarely in my life had I quit and when I had, the outcome of those situations had not been as good as first anticipated. I was not going to have my daughter find me sitting on the lounge starving and in a puddle of urine unable to make it to the bathroom and so I purchased a walking frame. My frame was like a faithful dog, always by my side only I never had to bother to feed it. It assisted in my journeys to the bathroom, to and from the kitchen and around my confined living space. I could not sit in the chair and give up on life. Edward had been dead for just over three years, he had given up on life and I would not do the same.

As time passed, it was evident that Claire was correct. On her last visit, she had again raised the subject of a retirement village. The most logical decision I could make would be to move. I was not keen on the idea, but who was I to argue with the science and art of sound reasoning. The fact was I knew I was not truly capable of looking after myself. In the last two years, I had incurred a broken wrist, was incapable of venturing upstairs. I was frequently forced to eat dry breakfast cereal for dinner, ashamed at the thought of phoning for help and unable to achieve any greater task. I could no longer bear to be a burden on my daughter and so I phoned Claire and asked her to make the appropriate arrangements.

Within two weeks, Claire had found a suitable retirement home. It was local, the rooms were very bright and airy, and access ramps were installed to make life easier. As we ventured around the grounds we passed other residents, their faces displayed smiles and that was a good sign.

At the Oakland Retirement Village, all residents had their own rooms equipped with telephone, panic buttons and private en-suites. Five nutritious meals were prepared daily; breakfast, lunch, dinner and both morning and afternoon tea. Monthly outings were organised for those who wished and general recreation sports such as lawn bowls, singing groups, darts and sewing classes were held on the premises. I was amazed. Never in my wildest dreams had I imagined that a retirement village could offer so much, so I signed all the papers and we arranged that I should move in the week after our meeting.

Once at the Oaklands, I began to put on weight and strength returned to my body. Then on one hot summer's day, I decided it was time to do something with my life. I would write a book, a book of my life, one, which revealed all. I had never disclosed all of my past to anyone and now was the time to do so, before it was too late. It was a transitional period of my life, the thought of commencing my writing made me nervous. I would have to confront the past, much of which was painful and made me feel shame. I decided that this book would remain a secret, only when it was completed and I was six foot under would I want anyone to read my tales. My life had a new meaning and a sense of urgency about finishing my book overwhelmed my body. I felt as though I was living on borrowed time and so I found an old typewriter. I was ready to begin. It would be appropriate to include details of my parents house which Claire knew nothing about. She would inherit this house and it was vital she knew the history which was attached.

The temperature outside had soared to unbelievable heights, everyone was indoors, and if I started now I would not be disturbed for hours. As I gazed out my window searching for the first vital words I noticed there were no birds in the sky or ants roaming the ground, I felt truly alone. Ideas for those first vital words whirled around in my head. This is a book about life, about my life, about the decisions I made, my actions and about consequences. My thoughts drifted to the meaning of life. From our very conception, many people have different ideas and beliefs on the meaning of life and so I began. From the moment I started the words continued to flow, it was as if the words were being drawn from me like the water being sucked out of a bath once the plug was removed.

I remained at my desk for the rest of the afternoon; at dinnertime I made a quick dash to the dining room, collected a sandwich and retreated to my room. I knew there would be many events that I would have to write about, many of which I had placed into the darkest corner of my mind, but all the same. Writing this book was something I had to achieve. For the weeks, following the greater percentage of my time was spent sitting at my desk, typing away and as I did so, I was overwhelmed by emotions. On some pages, I would find myself laughing, as I recalled events, while on others, my eyes could not contain my tears. Events from long ago came to mind easier than the events of recent times. I was alive, and as I relived the past I wondered about all the what ifs.

Liz, the lady who lived in the room next to me would tap on the window as she passed by for meals. I was lucky to have her as a reminder, otherwise, I probably would have stayed at my desk my typing only interrupted by toilet and drink breaks. Liz or Elizabeth as her family referred to her was a lovely lady. Throughout her life she had worked with many charities, she was a very religious woman and I envied the number of visitors she received. If she did not have a visitor every day then I would know something was wrong. Children, grandchildren, members from her church, the list of visitors went on and on. Liz would sit outside and smoke away, chatting to anyone who passed by. She was partially deaf, so I did not need to strain to hear most of her conversations. Before I started writing I would lay on my bed and listen. Her voice as loud as it was, was very comforting. Although she was not talking to me, I felt peace of mind knowing someone was close. When I commenced my writing, my view of her loud voice changed. She grated on my nerves and occasionally I had to restrain myself from yelling at her to shut up.

By the end of the month, my story was taking form. As I looked over my work in progress, I noticed that I have missed several events. In Chapter sixteen, which was when I was experiencing my depression after Aunt Kate died and Edward went to Melbourne I omitted to include that along with drinking, I was also smoking. I had smoked socially when I was younger, but never had I been addicted to the nicotine as I was when I was forty, way back in 1964. They did not have the patches, gum or those new inhaler things they have these days to help you quit, it was just cold turkey. I was not sure if it was the booze, the nicotine or the habit of both, which was more painful to stop. Now, as I recall those days, I am amazed that Edward did not sense the tension I felt.

I also omitted to include any great detail about Edward's death or funeral. I did mention that he retired after working for the same company for more than forty years. Well, after his retirement Edward appeared lost. Besides work, he had no outside interests and therefore I again raise the question of what does one do when they are financially secure and maybe even well respected but lack any real friends.

For Edward, retirement represented lonely days, reminiscing over past business successes. He did not know how to interact with others on a social level. His funeral was a sad occasion, for me it was not as bad as I had first feared. We had mutually separated years before and although we retained respect for one another, our love and affection had faded. For Claire, it was a different story; she lost a father whom in her younger years she never really knew. I was the one there when Claire hurt her finger, needed a band-aid or a bed time story read. Edward was always absent; he knew nothing about her personality likes or dislikes. Edward's extended work hours left little time for me and virtually no time for his daughter. I did not want or expect all of his time just a small percentage of pure quality time but he could not offer this to either of us.

In the years preceding Edward's death, Claire had discovered a closeness similar to the closeness she and I shared. That discovery was something, which pleased me, but still she had missed out on time that could never be recovered. Ben shared his mother's tears for he was losing his only grandfather, one who he truly adored. Although, I was not sure if at the age of nearly four Ben understood the concept of death he was aware he would never see his poppy again. I treasured the time I was with Edward, without him there would have been no Claire, Anthony or Ben. He gave me much joy and hope and while outwardly I expressed little emotion my silent thoughts, secret tears and precious memories kept Edward near both in life and after death. I would always have a special place in my heart for him, alone, a piece of life no one else could own.

You may have been wondering what happened to Stella, as I read over my story so far I notice that I have failed to make mention of her for some time.

After her move to Melbourne, Stella and I continued to remain close and she supported my every decision, never judging me. Above all else, the one thing that I wished for people was for happiness and Stella had found this with Sam in her new home of Melbourne. The news of my divorce upset her, but unlike many, she never laid blame. Sadly Stella died in 1985, she was a woman who I dearly loved and to this day, the thought of her passing still brings a tear to my eyes.

Well it is time for dinner now, today I am not having just a sandwich, as I have on many days since my writing began. Today is a baked dinner. I have been sitting here drooling for the last hour, listening to my stomach growl as the scrumptious smells of roasting pork and baked vegetables have wafted through my window. I am pleased with my achievements for today, so I think I will have a relaxing time and resume my writing after my well-deserved break. I am also going on a bus trip tomorrow, they have organised an outing to the Blue Mountains, and I have not been to the Blue Mountains for years, so the break will do me good.

The other day after writing about my smoking days, I asked Liz if I could cadge one of hers. Although she appeared shocked by my request, she was very obliging and handed me her packet along with her lighter. After about one minute of playing with her lighter trying to work out the child safety, I lit up. Well, now I know why I gave them up, I was coughing and spluttering everywhere, Liz jumped to her feet faster than I have ever seen her move and my smoking time was over faster than it had begun. Thanking Liz for the experience, I departed her company and returned to my room for a quick mouth rinse.At seventy-six years of age I decided I would not smoke again, not even for all the tea in China.

Oaklands is certainly living up to all the expectations; the only thing that I have missing in my life is company from the outside world. Claire visits almost every other week. Although lately, her visits have been closer to monthly than fortnightly. She is always very apologetic when she arrives. Generally, she brings Ben with her, with every visit, I see the changes in him, his vocabulary expands and he appears taller.He is nearly seven years old now and is in his first year of primary school. Already up to my shoulders, I imagine he will grow over six foot and take after his father, who himself is six and a half feet tall. All he talks about is being a fireman, his dreams of this career stemming from a visit to the local brigade. I am sure he will succeed in what ever he puts his mind to, the world has so much to offer for such a determined young lad.

Each night before I go to sleep, I pray for the health and safety of my family. I pray for peace. At my age, I can't change many things, I can only offer words and many times I am not so sure if my words could even be classified as words of wisdom. I try not to appear as a narrow-minded old lady. I know the world is changing, as too are the opinions of those around. From one generation to another there will always be a gap unless we all try to make bridges. We must all make the effort.

And so, I continue to write my story, the end is near, I must continue while I am able.

CHAPTER TWENTY-NINE

The fact is the only thing I can truly rely on these days, is this book and that is why it is so important to me. Friends, yes, I have friends, people who say they are friends. They promise to telephone. They promise to visit. To keep in contact. But, can I always rely on them to keep their promises? Nothing hurts more than a broken promise. This book, is something I can truly rely on.

My friends know who they are, they know what friendship we share, they know if I can rely on them. I hope they know what they mean to me.

I hope this book makes its readers reflect over their lives and the paths they choose to take. I hope it makes people think about what is really important.

You can never judge a book by its cover and you should never judge a person in that way either. We all come in different packages and that is important, otherwise, the world would be a boring place. Beauty is not only on the outside, it is not only skin deep. One's skin colour, one's body shape or size should not determine it. Pure beauty comes from within and radiates from within a person.

We are all just as important as the person next to us is. Our financial status, the job we have or do not have, where we live, what car we drive, our outward appearance or whom we choose to sleep with does not determine who we are, who we really are. If you judge a person by these things then you should expect to be judged in the same manner. You can not judge a person until you have walked a mile in their shoes.

Accept people for who they are. I am not saying you have to agree with everything or everyone. But, if you accept others and learn to love unconditionally, then, you will realise how much more life has to offer.

You can not change another person in this world. You may be able to influence them, but you can never change a person. The only person you can change is yourself. I only wish I had received similar advice when I was much younger, I only wish I had been able to accept all people. My life would have been so much happier, my life did not turn out how I expected, life does not always do that.

And now, it is time to let the cat out of the bag as they say. The end of my story is near and I owe you, the truth, the complete truth. For words do not have to be spoken to form a lie and holding onto secrets in it self can sometimes be extremely destructive. Especially, when they could be classed as deep and dark.

Remember, sometimes in life, not all is what it seems.

Friday 22nd December 1939, was a particularly strange day from the moment I woke, in the early hours. Wiping the sleep from my eyes, I yawned and as I gained focus, I watched the shadows cast by the branches of the tree outside, embrace my room like outstretched arms. The streetlights were still on, although, they would soon be extinguished as the sun was struggling to infiltrate the darkness. Inside my bedroom, the air around felt quite thick. As if a cloud was hanging over me. With summer here, I knew we were going to have another hot day. This heat would only add to the frustration of all. It was time for me to act, to do something. However, what? I did not know what but I could no longer bear to endure the feelings of hopelessness, which seemed to follow our every move. I was sure there was a solution; a relief if not only temporary had to be within my reach. All I had to do was to think. And so, as I listened to the sobbing which echoed down the hallway from my parent's room, I lay in the softness of my bed and began to conjure up ideas.

My first thought, was a holiday; we could all take a trip to Dunberry. My parents always voiced how relaxing our holidays had been. I was a genius. At breakfast, I would tell my parents of my idea and they too would share my smile. They too, would feel the instant relief, the happy thought of an escape. I stretched my arms upward from beneath the covers then threw my fists down beside my body, *Damn!* As fast as my happy solution had come to mind, it was gone. I recalled my father's complaints about his work commitments during the Christmas period, this genius idea was not possible and so I continued to rack my brain.

The lingering noise of my mother's sobbing continued. This was not unusual; my mother had become very emotional over the past months. It was as if the strain of the Depression and the lingering thought of the war were taking its toll. For as long as I could remember mum would experience what dad referred to as *episodes*. Mum would randomly cry at the drop of a hat, lose interest in nearly everything and remain in bed for days stating she was ill, although she did not have any symptoms of a cold or flu. Dad would instruct me to keep noise to a minimum and warn me that it would be better if I just steered clear when she was like that. Sometimes, I could tell when an *episode* was approaching. She would become extremely sensitive and snappy, while her appetite would increase. Every time I looked at her, she was like a cow chewing its cud, continually munching away. Dad would fuss around, telling her that things were all good, picking up objects, she left laying around and assisting with the household duties and sometimes, this would work. However, recently this approach had not worked and it appeared everything and everyone was getting on top of her. Dad and I included and I could tell that her overwhelming feeling of sadness was also effecting dad. Piles of dirty clothes were left in the laundry; the kitchen sink held an increasing number of plates, cups and pots that were yet to be washed. At night mum increasingly retreated to her bedroom straight after dinner, till such time she didn't bother to come out, unless she needed to use the bathroom. Dad was extremely concerned and seemed at a loss as to what he could do. Confiding in me, he said he felt as though everything was crumbling and falling apart. Suggesting I could ask old Mrs. Sharp for her advice, dad hit the roof demanding I keep my mouth shut.

"What happens in this family stays in this family!"

He paused for a moment, then continued while glaring at me and pointing his finger within inches of my face.

"Do you want to bring shame to our family name?" his voice raised and abrupt. Shaking my head, I replied, "No!" And that was that, I could say no more.

Beside mum's *episodes*, both my parents had generally been happy individuals, comfortable with most situations. However, by the time this day arrived, they had their comfort zones stripped from them. Their reaction to the situation at that time could have been compared to the reaction of an individual who had been thrown naked onto a crowded street. The events which were occurring outside our front door were infiltrating the security of our lives, destroying happiness and hope, infusing slowly into our minds gloom, doom and vulnerability. My mother had visited our family doctor back in November and had been prescribed medication to assist in sleeping. It was a somewhat drastic measure; but then again, I know only too well, how drastic times can result in drastic measures.

Chloral Hydrate and Potassium Bromide were the drugs of the day. Potassium Bromide at the time was a standard treatment for epilepsy, however, being a depressant of the central nervous system, it was also used as sedative because it depressed reflexes and produced drowsiness. Chloral Hydrate was equal in popularity. Although it possessed an unpleasant taste, this chemical cocktail was rapidly absorbed from the stomach and produced its effects within half an hour, which would see an individual sleeping soundly within minutes of ingestion. A temporary measure used to escape the world outside.

That was it. That was my solution. I would make my parents breakfast in bed, into my creation I would add a little of both drugs. Mixed in with scrambled eggs, juice and coffee they would not detect its presence and after eating, they would drift back to sleep. A day sleeping in bed with complete relaxation would improve their thoughts; it was just what the doctor ordered.My mother always said to me when I was not feeling well that there was nothing better than a good day's rest in bed to clear away my blues. And so, I clambered out of bed threw on my dressing gown and proceeded downstairs to the kitchen.

With my ingenious idea, I began creating the breakfast of all breakfasts. Humming as I whisked the eggs, I added small amounts of the sedatives, with additional sprinkles for the extra touch. The air around me no longer felt thick, the smell of freshly brewed coffee carried with it hope that I was somehow capable of relieving my parents pain. Preparing a breakfast tray, I served the eggs onto plates, poured the coffee and juice and proceeded towards my parent's room.

Knocking on their door and announcing myself as room service, I went in. I could tell by their reaction that my creation was very unexpected yet a pleasant surprise. My mother wiped her teary eyes and sat up. With open arms and words of praise, they both accepted the breakfast I prepared and consumed it without even one word of suspicion regarding its hidden ingredients. From the side of their bed, I ate some toast covered with peanut butter and honey then once they were finished I gathered their tray and took it back to the kitchen. My plan was working perfectly, and so as I began to clean up all this dishes in the kitchen including the mess I had created, grinning at my success.

Bugsy had departed our company in the late hours of the previous night. He had been staying out at Parramatta, where he had found temporary work Glass, Balls and Company. We had laughed about not only the name of the company but also his boss who was inappropriately named, Dick Rootinbrake. Bestowing such an atrocious name on an individual would surely be the result of either an unwanted pregnancy or one ugly baby. Bugsy had stated they were not even lucky enough to have a coffee break, let a lone a rooting break. He liked to see me smile and was always making up jokes to make my laugh.I could tell he sensed my unhappiness and so as he wrapped his arms around me, he assured me that things would be all right. His strong arms and warm embrace gave me hope, hope held together by fond memories we both shared of happier times.

Now I had added to this hope, my parents would have a relaxing day in bed and would wake up feeling refreshed. Wanting to share my happiness I phoned Bugsy at Glass, Balls and Company and advised him of my actions. Unlike myself, Bugsy did not agree in the wisdom of my actions and began to question the quantity of the drugs I had added. A level of concern was evident in his voice, as he insisted that he come over straight away to ensure everything was all right. Hanging up the receiver I began to doubt my actions, from upstairs there was no noise. Had I in fact given my parents an overdose? A cold shiver travelled up my spine as I read the instructions on both bottles, with a sprinkle here and a sprinkle there of each I was not sure if I had in fact added well past the recommended dosage. My breathing became rapid, as I nervously approached the stairs, looking towards the top. I was relieved to see my mother standing there. She had not suffered an overdose, she was not dead, she was alive and I was overwhelmed with relief.

Reaching out towards the handrail, she appeared somewhat drowsy. Then, as she was about to begin on her first step, it all happened. Like a sack of potatoes she came tumbling down, thud after thud after thud until finally she lay at my feet. After a few groans, which lasted several seconds her body lay motionless, her legs twisted in ways I had never thought possible, her neck turned with her head on the side and from her right ear I could see blood. I stared in horror, frozen in a state of shock.

What had I done?

From the top of the stairs, there came the voice of

my father. He would surely beat me until I could no longer sit down. Dad never believed in accidents. I was trembling as he emerged from the bedroom; he too appeared drowsy and disorientated, his motor responses slower than usual. Upon seeing my mother's body, he proceeded down the stairs. His body swaying from side to side, his voice raised questioning what I had done. Reaching the bottom he dropped to the ground and grabbed my mother's shoulders. He was pleading for her to respond, but she did not.

"What have you done to me, what have you done?"

His eyes rolled around as he tried to focus his anger on me. It was obvious the drugs were taking an effect, not the effect I had anticipated but an effect, which I could never have conceived, not even in my worst nightmare.

"You killed her…You killed your mother…You're trying to kill me!"

His speech was slurred; words were not as pronounced as they usually were.

"You will go to jail…You will be in jail for the rest of your life…You ungrateful little girl."

He began to thrash his arms towards me.

"Come here, I'll teach you."

All I could think of was being locked up in jail for the rest of my life, I could not do that, I would not cope. My father's hand grabbed my ankle and with one quick swoop I snatched the vase from the hallway stand and swung it as hard as I could in his direction. Hitting him fair in the side of his head, he collapsed to the floor. Both my parents' bodies lay motionless at my feet. Too afraid to confirm what I suspected I stood in numbness, stupefied by the preceding events. My entire body struck senseless, my feet feeling as though they were contained within concrete blocks. The only noise was that of my breathing. I was panting like a dog, which had been on an exhausting run. Feeling as though a tight rope had been bound around my chest restricting every breath, I took.

I am not sure how much time had passed, when Bugsy made it to my place, the streetlights had long been extinguished. My parent's bodies both remained motionless. Although, I had managed to roll them over and drag them next to the wall, so I could clean up the mess they had made. I could not bear to look at the blood and I certainly didn't want anyone else to see any signs of it. I did not want anyone to see any trace of what had transpired. Getting rid of the blood was crucial and so with a bucket, scrubbing brush, damp cloth followed by a dry rag I scrubbed, washed and wiped down the immediate area until such time no traces of blood remained. With their heads cushioned by folded up towels to absorb the blood, they appeared peaceful as they lay out on their backs next to each other. Hands comfortably resting on their abdomens, clothes straightened and legs crossed at their ankles. It was just as if they were sleeping. Bugsy bashed on the front door that hard I thought he was going to come straight through it. Embracing him in my arms, I cried hysterically.

"They fell. They both fell. Like sacks of potatoes. They fell from the top of the stairs. It was an accident. It was all an accident."

Grabbing my arms, he forced me to release him. Staring directly into my eyes, he then looked beyond my shaking body. From the expression on his face, I could tell Bugsy was not at all shocked by his discovery, or maybe he was simply scared witless.

"Oh shit! Oh shit! Oh shit!" he exclaimed.

Immediately, he began telling me of how he could assist in the disposal of their bodies. It was as if he knew he would find them dead. Taking me by the shoulders he told me, it was no time to stand still. We would have to act and act fast. No jury would believe my recollection of events and there was no way that he would want to see me imprisoned for an accident such as it was.

Taking me by the hand he led me to the garden shed, where he quickly took hold of a pick and shovel then he dragged me back to the house. At the driveway side of the house was a small doorway which led underneath, Bugsy explained to me how we would dig a hole and dispose of my parents' bodies. Prior to that day we had used under the house as a hiding place when he visited; lit with candles we would sit under there for hours and discuss our lives. If we acted fast enough no one would suspect a thing, no one would know the truth of what happened and I would not go to jail.

It took hours to dig the hole, Bugsy did most of the digging, he dug on pure adrenalin as I sat watching and staring into space like a zombie. What started out as an ingenious plan for my parents to escape their feeling of sadness had developed into a nightmare with catastrophic results. Bugsy assured me that my secret would remain with him. He was my knight in shining armour.

When the digging was completed, it was time to collect my parents' bodies. As I sit here now and reflect back over the event, I am not sure what I felt. Shock would have to be a word that best described the moment. I never dreamed the consequences of my actions could be so devastating and as we walked back into the house, I don't really think I fully comprehended what was happening. First, we went to the side of my mother. Bugsy instructed me to take her by the feet; he gently lifted her head and took a hold of her from behind around under her arms. Together we carried her outside and under the house where we laid her body next to the hole. Then it was time to collect my fathers body, carrying him out to the hole was a more difficult task, his size and weight had me gasping for breath as I struggled not to let go. Laying his body next to my mother's we sat and rested for a second before lowering them into what would be their grave. Mother's body went in first then father's body went in, looking down on them they appeared to be sleeping. My father was partially on his side; one arm over my mother's chest. They both looked so peaceful.

Bugsy reached for the shovel and started to fill the hole, he was instructing me to pull myself together. Although, I could hear his words I sat there in silence, trying to come to terms with what was happening. It was as if I were in a dream, a nightmare was unfolding before my eyes and there was nothing I could do to escape it. As the dirt went in tears welled in my eyes, first their legs disappeared, then their torsos. *Goodbye Mum and Dad, may you rest in peace.* I looked around wondering if their spirits were hovering overhead. I wondered what they were thinking. Then from the depths of the hole came a noise. It sounded as if it were a moan. Bugsy stopped shovelling and we both peered in. There was no movement. I could feel a lump in my throat. Were they still alive? Were we burying my parents alive? After a few seconds Bugsy resumed shovelling. Soon after, all visibility of my parents had gone. They were now under about six-foot of dirt. They were now gone. Their suffering was over. I had to come to grips with my actions, only memories remained.

Over the burial site, Bugsy stacked a large mound of firewood, which he decided would be best to relocate from within the garden shed. This he explained would hide evidence of recently upturned soil below. Once the timber reached waist height he collected the shovel and pick then stood silently beside me, placing his arm around my waist he assured me that our actions were justifiable. My intentions had been good, non-violent, it was purely an accident. What I did to my father was not premeditated; he had provoked the situation with his attempted attack and threats. Cleaning up after the aftermath, the disposing of the bodies had been our only solution to the situation.

I stood motionless and said my silent good-byes. I also apologised. I wanted my parents to know that I had never intended to inflict pain. It was only ever my intention to eliminate their suffering. I wanted them to know I loved them. I wanted them to know what I had felt. Again, I looked around wondering if my parent's spirits were hovering above, if so, what they were thinking.

After a short while, I took Bugsy's hand and turned my back on the unmarked grave, I never looked back. I never laid my eyes on that site again.

CHAPTER THIRTY

The irony of all the angst, regarding my parents disappearance all those years ago, is that while on the outside I displayed a face of sadness and heartache, seemingly an inconsolable fifteen year old. Inwardly, I experienced a feeling of overwhelming calm, as if a huge weight had been lifted from my shoulders. I would no longer have to endure watching my parents suffer. What started out as the perfect plan to create a temporary relief for them both had gone terribly wrong, yet, with all that, I could still reason with myself and view my actions as the ultimate escape, something good. My parents would no longer suffer and I had made this escape from all suffering possible, intentional or not.

My parents had set in place a strict regime. Ensuring I lived my life in accordance with the rules they set, which ensured all required tasks were accomplished. I was punished for my untidiness, my insubordination and for my slow response to their requests. I had my wardrobe stripped of its contents on more than one occasion due to the disorder; I had my mouth washed out with soap on more than one occasion due to the words I spoke. I had my behind whipped with my fathers leather belt on more than one occasion as well.

Yet, still all these years later I can not pinpoint the one reason for my initiating a plan, which would see the ultimate demise of my parents, my creators, those who had begotten a baby daughter. Maybe, it was due to my immaturity, that I could not understand nor accept that throughout our lives there is much suffering. These days I can appreciate that in life we must suffer and experience bad times so we can appreciate the good. These days, I would say if you want advice on life then speak to someone who has lived.

All those years ago, I had displayed a very convincing facade that was of award winning performance quality. I was never suspected to be linked to my parent's disappearance. There were routine questions of course; when did I last see them? What were they wearing? Had there been an argument? But never, did they ask me if I had anything to do with their disappearance. As far as anyone could work out, both woke up, showered, dressed, ate breakfast and went for an early morning stroll, from which they never returned.

I was whisked away to my aunt Kate's to live until I finished my schooling; I was a model student - Straight A's. Aunt Kate, dad's sister lived near by in Paddington. I heard them, my two aunts and a welfare officer, talking the day after my parents disappearance was reported to the police. Behind closed doors, with no input from me, it was decided where I would live. Not that the decision bothered me. Aunt Kate lived in close proximity to all my regular haunts; my aunt Margaret lived in Newcastle.

However, the location of my aunt's residence wasn't the underlying factor of my preference, it was the fact my parents had always considered her the black sheep of the family. She had never married. A professional artist; her paintings attracted buyers both nationally and internationally, she was a successful working female without a husband; a concept my parents never understood. My parents were too undiscerning and ignorant to acknowledge her as they did others within our family - not because of her never married status but because she led a bohemian lifestyle. Oh, how ignorance and that good old "bury your head in the sand" mentality can get in the way of or ruin a relationship.

I wondered if my parents thought about those sorts of things in their last dying moments. I wondered if my parents thought about all those "what if" scenarios which frequently infiltrated our minds. I wondered if only for one second, they thought of Aunt Kate, as I am sure you would think of your family, friends, life experiences and incomplete dreams.

I needed Aunt Kate; I needed to be with someone of such independence and individualism. It was her open-mindedness, her understanding, her acceptance of others and her unconditional love, which made her seem worlds apart from my parents. I had escaped their world, a huge weight had been lifted from my shoulders with their passing, now it was time to enter a world full of feelings and attitudes I had rarely seen, yet, longed to openly experience.

I suppose you are wondering, how a fifteen year-old could be involved in her parent's disappearance. Doubting the truth behind my words, I never said the results of my actions were intentional. But, believe me this story is true, I also never said I accomplished this task alone and I know it wouldn't have been the same if Bugsy hadn't helped, if he hadn't come to my rescue. All those years ago Bugsy had participated in this unspeakable crime and his participation was due to his feelings for me, his feeling had overridden all sense of sensibility. Following his heart instead of his head, his feelings for me had persuaded him into thinking his participation was for the best.

To Bugsy, I was a temptress; I had him twisted around my little finger; if I said jump, he would say how high. Blinded by his feelings for me he participated in this unspeakable act, wanting to please. They say love is blind and how true it is. Bugsy was blinded by his love and once he realised those feelings were not reciprocated, Bugsy was no more. They said it was a car accident, however, I suspected it was much more. Guilt is a very consuming feeling that most of us experience at some point in our lives. Bugsy couldn't live with his.

I had tried to kill and destroy all the wrong and suffering in the world. I had thought my parents silently wished for their untimely fate. I couldn't bear to see all the wrong in the world, all the heartache, all the pain, all the unhappiness. I didn't know what I could do to make things right, what I could do to make people more than just content in their lives.

"You are an unaffectionate person." That is something someone dear, once said to me. Although, I do not believe there is such a word, I certainly understood the intended meaning. I sit here, my fingers slowly striking the keyboard, at times unable to keep up with the momentum of my thoughts. I am not an affectionate person. Then, what am I? I know what I want to be. I know what I can be. But, from an outsider, I am not?

I am not the person I had fooled myself into thinking I was. I am just as common as the person next to me. No more, no less… Or maybe less, maybe I should even consider myself evil, do you? Not everyone in the world destroys those close to them just because they don't agree with the words they speak or because they don't like what they see. I have done so much wrong in my life and I have fooled those close to me into thinking it was me who was experiencing rather than creating the suffering, which surrounded me.

The anguish and shame I have felt at times was so overwhelming I silently prayed I would be exposed for who I really was. I prayed as I went to bed that I would not wake in the morning. A prisoner trapped within my own thoughts, trapped by my unspeakable actions, like a spider stuck in its own web, spun so tightly that no matter what I did I could not escape my web of past actions.

With the wisdom I have derived, through the course of my life I sit here, a frail lonely old cadaverous woman. My hands crippled by time, swollen and monstrous, the result of arthritis.Yes, throughout my life I had thought by ending the existence of those suffering around me or by destroying those who hurt me I would feel better, I would feel a weight lift from my shoulders. And yes, that feeling was experienced for a short period. However, it soon disappeared, replaced by remorse and guilt for those past wrongdoings. For over sixty long years remorse and guilt have shadowed my every move, my every thought.

Tolerance and acceptance are two very important words, two very important qualities a person should possess. Two things, I had missing in my younger years. I cannot undo things, which have been done. I cannot undo words, which have been spoken. Yes, I can regret all these things but I can never take them back and so I will leave you with one last thing…

Pages Of Your Life

Life is so precious when born it's a blank book of stories not yet told,
Make sure you fill your pages before you get too old,
As your pages turn into chapters that's when memories begin to form,
Some will be happy others sad, some cold and others warm.

Friends and families enter into chapters and in others they disappear,
Nights roll into days, weeks, months and chapters into years,
So, learn from your mistakes in pages that have past,
Try to make your first be your very last,

Treat people with respect, the way you want to treated in return,
For when you look back on your chapters that's when you really learn,
Make sure you live your life safely as one chance is all you've got,
Closing your book before you're ready is definitely not what you want.

Your book now full of experiences with fewer blank pages still to live,
Make the best of your pages; make sure the best is what you give.

www.ingramcontent.com/pod-product-compliance
Lightning Source LLC
Chambersburg PA
CBHW021004120726
47905CB00009B/2854